COME
HIGH WATER

A Black Swan Historical Romance

COME HIGH WATER

•

Carolyn Brown

AVALON BOOKS
NEW YORK

Published by Thomas Bouregy & Co., Inc.
160 Madison Avenue, New York, NY 10016

Library of Congress Cataloging-in-Publication Data

Brown, Carolyn, 1948–
    Come high water / Carolyn Brown.
        p. cm.   (A black swan historical romance ; no. 3)
      ISBN 978-0-8034-7766-7 (acid-free paper)
1. Hotelkeepers—Fiction.   2. Veterans—Fiction.
3. Arkansas—Fiction.   I. Title.
    PS3552.R685275C66 2010
    813'.54—dc22
                                                    2010002299

PRINTED IN THE UNITED STATES OF AMERICA
ON ACID-FREE PAPER
BY HADDON CRAFTSMEN, BLOOMSBURG, PENNSYLVANIA

For many years of
continuing to believe in me, this book is for
Ellen Mickelsen.

Chapter One

If it could go wrong, it did.

If it couldn't go wrong, it did anyway.

That's what caused Bridget O'Shea to grab her coat and umbrella and storm out of the Black Swan hotel that bitterly cold January afternoon. A petite lady with a mass of strawberry blond hair piled on top of her head, her features were delicate—small nose, a rosebud mouth made for kissing, and blue eyes that danced when she was happy but could cut steel when she was angry. That morning they could cut steel.

All because of a blasted rat, cornering her in the kitchen like that. She hated anything or anyone able to take all the control from her. Her ex-husband, Ralph Contiello, had ripped every shred of self-worth from her with his abusiveness during the year they were married.

1

Once he was gone from her life, she'd vowed that no one would ever make her cringe in a corner again while a belt slapped against her hide. And now a simple rat had brought back all those emotions. It hadn't held a razor strop in its paws when it reared up on its hind legs and glared at her with those beady little eyes, but it had evoked the exact same measure of helplessness.

"Where would you be heading off to in such a hurry?" Major Engram asked from the front porch steps. Bundled up in a coat over his faded and patched bib overalls, with a hat pulled low on his head to shed the rain, he had a face full of wrinkles and a kind smile in his bright eyes. One of the oldest citizens in Huttig, he enjoyed the food and the visiting at the Black Swan. Besides, he could always depend on a blaze in the massive fireplace to warm his hands by.

"I'm going to the train station. Come hell or high water, I'm bringing a man back to work for me," she said.

"Sounds like a good thing to me, Miss Bridget. You should've gotten someone when your sister stayed in Mississippi last month. This is too much for you and Allie Mae to run by y'alls' selves. You need a man to help you. I'd apply for the job, but you need someone young and strong," he said. "I'll just go on down to the Commercial for a cup of coffee this morning."

"You'd best do just that, Major. The coffee isn't made, and I'm mighty poor company," she said.

After the ordeal with Ralph last year, she didn't trust men, but she was wise enough to realize that the hotel needed someone with brawn and brains to boot—someone to do the heavy work, manage the front desk, and kill a rat the size of a pregnant house cat. She didn't care if the man was as ugly as a mud fence; she wasn't husband hunting and never would be again. She'd learned her lesson the hardest way possible the first time Ralph Contiello came home and found his water glass on the wrong side of his dinner plate. Her husband was barely a step up from a garden slug. At least it wasn't against the law to kill a slug. Too bad it wasn't the same for husbands. All she wanted was a muscular man who could work and didn't give her any sass concerning taking orders from a woman.

There had been three O'Shea sisters at the Black Swan when the great flu epidemic of 1918 claimed her father and mother, and then everything went to hell in a hand-basket. Catherine, the oldest and the strongest, would have been able to take care of that rat. She would have either shot it between the eyes or simply scared it to death with one of her get-out-of-here looks. But she'd married the very detective the Contiellos had sent looking for Ralph when he went missing. Alice, the middle sister, would have given the rat a blank, I-don't-even-know-you-are-there look; then, when the rat decided that Alice was harmless and turned its back, she would have beaten it to death with a broom. Afterward she would have made tea and ignored the dead carcass while she ate cookies and painted a picture of a tulip. But Alice had married Catherine's fiancé, who'd come back from the dead.

Bridget, the youngest O'Shea, might not be able to do a blessed thing about a vicious rat, but she knew how to hire help.

Nowadays Catherine lived in Little Rock with her new husband, Quincy, and Alice was settling in on a farm in Grace, Mississippi, with the love of her life, Ira. That left Bridget in Huttig, Arkansas, with a hotel to run and a rat that thought it owned her kitchen.

So, come hell or high water, she intended to hire a man to work at the Black Swan. With the downpour of rain beating against her umbrella, she wasn't so sure the high water wouldn't arrive before Lucifer's flames. She had bragged to her sisters, Catherine and Alice, that she could run the Black Swan single-handedly when they expressed doubts about getting married and leaving her alone in Huttig. And she could run it—with one more hired hand. It had taken all three of them to run the hotel after their parents died—Catherine, Alice, and Bridget. And when she hired one more person, there would be three again. She had been wise enough to hire Allie Mae to help in the kitchen and take care of the bedrooms after Alice married Ira. The two of them had managed for a month to keep the Black Swan going without a hitch, but Allie Mae was as afraid of rats as Bridget was.

That big gray varmint with a hairless tail would stop threatening her when she found the biggest man at the train station to come kill it. Then there would be three people to work the hotel again, and everything would be just fine.

"He doesn't even have to be smart. I don't care if he can figure amounts for meals or rents. Forget the brains. I can do the books and handle the money. I need someone with great big feet to kick a rat plumb across the state and even the Mississippi River. God, I hate rats almost as much as I grew to hate Ralph Contiello," she mumbled as she walked.

"Good morning, Bridget." Her next door neighbor, Mabel, appeared right in front of her. "Who are you talking to, and what are you doing out so early? I've been to the grocery store and put in my order for the week. Good thing we brought our umbrellas, isn't it? Are you going to answer me, or are you going to stand there and stare like your simple sister, Alice, used to do?"

Bridget wished that shaking her head would make the woman disappear. She tried it, just in case, but it didn't work. "Excuse me. I was talking to myself. Have a nice day, Mabel."

She hurried around the woman who held the title of biggest gossip in Union County, Arkansas, leaving her standing there with her mouth hanging open.

Mabel stomped her foot, only to send a spray of water up around her hem. Her long, skinny nose twitched at the mud she'd have to wash from her dress, and her thin mouth, set in a bed of wrinkles, tightened up to no more than a disgusted line across her irritated face. "Well, I never!"

"Something wrong?" Lydia Jones asked from so close behind her that Mabel jumped. Lydia was a friend of sorts, a relative of the gossip bloodline and a wizened little lady in a black dress, her withered face peeping out from under her austere black umbrella.

Mabel went into an instant and well-known tirade. "Them O'Sheas is all touched. Their momma named them right. Catherine for the earth, and, goodness knows, she wallowed in the dirt and ruined her reputation, the way she acted with that private detective. And Alice for air. I still don't know why in the name of sweet Jesus Ira McNewell married such a dimwit. And Bridget for water. She don't know if she's coming or going, she's so unstable. And to think of her trying to run that hotel by herself! What a crazy notion."

"Scandalous!" Lydia murmured and kept walking beside her.

Bridget could have cared less if they discussed her or her sisters. Neither woman understood what had gone on the past year at the Black Swan. Sometimes she wasn't so sure she did either, and she'd lived through it all.

The morning train from the north had just come to a screeching halt when Bridget arrived at the station. Men of every size and description streamed out the doors. The war was over, and work was scarce. Every day more and more came to southern Arkansas hoping to find work at the sawmill. They stayed a day or less when they discovered that the mill wasn't hiring and had, in fact, cut back on help since the war's end just months before.

Bridget kept her head down, looking at the ex-soldiers' feet. None of them looked big enough to kill the rat. She felt someone's eyes on her and glanced up, only to find a man leering at her with the same kind of eyes her ex-husband had. That worthless lump of flesh would never see the inside of her hotel. Besides, his feet were too blamed small to kill the rat, which had grown in her mind to twice its original size since she left the hotel.

"What you looking for, lady?" the man asked, showing off a mouthful of tobacco-stained teeth.

"Just waiting on someone," she answered.

"You here to find a man? I got a few dollars, if that's what your line of work is," he said.

"I'm here waiting for someone. I just told you that. So if you'll move aside and let me get into the station where it's warm, I would appreciate it. And this is a family town, so if you're looking for women like that, you've come to the wrong place," she said.

"You're a looker, you are. You change your mind, you just whistle right loud, and I'll come runnin' with money in hand."

She shuddered but kept walking.

Not one man looked trustworthy. Not a single one. Finally she gave up and went inside the station for a bit of warmth before heading back to the hotel to tell Allie Mae they'd have to find a rat trap and set it themselves. She'd wait until the varmint was in the trap and graveyard dead to tell Allie Mae that she had to dispose of it.

There was no way Bridget would ever touch it. When her father was living, he took care of any stray rat that made its way into the hotel. In the past two years they hadn't seen a single one, and Bridget had entertained notions that the flu had struck them as well as the human population of Huttig, Arkansas. Evidently one had survived to bring terror to Bridget, but she would get rid of it one way or another. She might even drag out the gun. A vision of the night she'd shot at Ralph and missed played through her mind. How could she hit a rat if she couldn't pop the spawn of Lucifer through the head?

"I wouldn't be nearly as afraid, and I could dang sure aim better," she huffed.

Wyatt Ferguson was headed home to Alvord, Texas, after weeks on the road. He was tired to the bone, but he danged sure wasn't looking forward to reaching his destination. Not with the situation what it was in Alvord. In six weeks it would all be over, but if he went home now he'd be the saddest, most depressed man alive in the midst of a whole string of parties. There didn't seem to be a way out of it, however, so he sighed and picked up a paper lying beside him on the bench.

He was busy reading an article in the three-month-old newspaper about the Elaine, Arkansas, massacre and didn't even see the petite red-haired lady open the door. It wasn't until she sat down beside him and whipped the scarf from around her head that he realized there was a woman in the station. When he noticed the mass of strawberry blond hair escaping the pins trying desperately to keep it confined in a tidy bun, she was looking at his feet.

Slowly her eyes traveled upward over every inch of his body in a way that made him squirm. It was a slow inspection, passing his trim waist, silver belt buckle, wide chest, steely blue eyes, and even the frown on his face, not stopping until he figured she'd counted every curly blond hair on his head. Heat warmed his neck as she sized him up.

She was either a woman of the evening out entirely too early in the day, or else she was an idiot completely devoid of any social skills. Women—not even in the modern world of 1920—did not scrutinize a man that way. It simply was not done.

He'd never been attracted to tiny women, rather liking those who were tall, well-rounded, and full-bosomed. And he'd hated red hair from the day he started school and Sally Ann McDay whipped him soundly. She'd had freckles, red hair, and brown eyes, and from that day to the present he'd steered clear of such women. So there was nothing about this woman to interest him, no matter what or who she was. Her most redeeming quality was her big, rounded, blue-green eyes.

"You'll do nicely," the woman said.

"Nicely for what?" he asked.

"It's plain you are here looking for sawmill work. It's what all the men come to Huttig for—work. Well, I'll save you some time. They aren't hiring. Haven't been in months. They laid off the extra help when the war was over. So you, like all these other hoboes around this station, are out of luck. I'll pay you a dollar a day plus room and board," she said.

He raised an eyebrow. "Such high wages?"

"Take it or leave it. There's lots of men out here who'd be glad to have it."

"And what would be my duties in this dollar-a-day job?" he asked.

"You do whatever I tell you to do. I own and operate the Black Swan hotel. We have a small restaurant and eight upstairs rooms to rent out. The first job you'll have is killing a rat in my kitchen."

"And to whom do you let the rooms upstairs?" he asked. He'd be damned if he'd take on a job that would land him in jail for aiding and abetting in something illegal.

"Whoever needs to rest for a night. You can have whichever room you want as part of your salary. Sometimes we have traveling salesmen. Sometimes it's a family just wanting to get off the train for a few days before moving on. The Swan has a wonderful reputation both as a hotel and as a restaurant."

Wyatt came close to laughing aloud, but the lady looked so serious. He hadn't been amused in weeks— months, if he was honest. He had two hours before the next train south would take him on home to Alvord, Texas, so he might as well follow the lady back to her hotel and kill a rat for her. After all, she didn't have a single freckle on her delicate little face, her hair wasn't really red, and her big, round eyes were the most fantastic shade of aqua he'd ever seen. It would be a lot more fun than sitting in the station watching ex-soldiers getting off the train and others boarding.

He stood, and Bridget wondered if his head would scrape the ceiling, he was so tall. He ran his fingers through his blond hair before settling a brown felt hat on his head at a jaunty angle. The overcoat he slipped into looked expensive, and she wondered what he was doing in Huttig looking for sawmill work if he could afford such a coat, but the notion flitted in and out of her mind without staying long.

"Get your baggage," she said.

He shook his head. "I'll take a look at this job you're offering me. If I like it, I'll come back for my trunk. If not, I won't have toted it for nothing."

"Fair enough," she said.

"And where is this hotel?" he asked after they'd walked along in silence for a half a mile. Suddenly he wondered if he'd just let himself be roped into a scam. The lady was the bait. A gang of bandits could be waiting to rob or kill him in the tall pine trees covering every inch of space that hadn't been claimed for a small house or business. Wyatt Ferguson could easily be left with nothing to take back to the train station but his long johns when they finished with him.

"Just a little farther. I forgot to ask your name."

"Wyatt Ferguson."

"Where are you from?"

"Alvord, Texas. And who are you?"

"I'm Bridget O'Shea. My parents came here when I was just a little girl, back when Huttig was being put up as a town. Seventeen years ago. My father built the Black Swan hotel. He named it that because a black swan with uplifted wings set inside a circle has something to do with his family, the O'Sheas, in Ireland. It's on the door and on the sign out front. The black swan is our good-luck symbol."

That explanation eased his imagination concerning walking through town barefoot in nothing but his underwear. When the hotel appeared through the trees, the tension in his muscles relaxed completely. Likely he'd get back to the station fully dressed and with a tall tale to tell his four brothers in Alvord.

The sign in the front yard proclaimed the building to be the Black Swan Hotel and Restaurant. It didn't look as if it warranted such a fine name. Actually, it looked more like a nice-sized home. Painted pristine white, it had a wide porch, complete with rocking chairs. He could imagine the place in the spring, with the now-dormant rosebushes blooming, a cool breeze fluffing the fronds of ferns hanging in baskets, and conversation rippling among the patrons as the rocking chairs creaked. Yes, it would be a cozy little hideaway on the outskirts of Huttig.

She marched onto the porch in front of him, swung wide the door, and left it open for him. "I've hired some help, Allie Mae," she announced. "Is the critter still in the kitchen?"

"No, ma'am. It run out here and under the settee— the red one over there in front of the fireplace. I been watchin' it close so it don't climb up here and hurt Miss Ella."

Wyatt stopped just inside the door and took stock of the room. A huge fireplace with a crackling blaze covered one wall. Lace curtains let in all the light offered on a cold January morning. Cheerful daisy wallpaper covered the walls. Furniture was arranged to take advantage of the space in the large lobby. An archway to his right led into a restaurant, and a doorway straight ahead went into a living space that he immediately figured was the family's private quarters. A stairway to his left went up to the eight rooms Bridget O'Shea had talked about.

The hotel clerk's area jutted out at an angle from the restaurant archway, making it easy to collect payment for dinner or supper as well as to do business for the upstairs rooms. A pretty young girl sat cross-legged on top of the clerk's desk, a sleeping baby cradled in her arms. Allie Mae had long, light brown hair braided into two ropes hanging down her back, a sprinkling of freckles across her pert nose, and brown eyes. She wore a blue cotton dress with a white bib apron over it, and if she was a day over fifteen, Wyatt would sprinkle salt on his dirty socks and have them for lunch.

"What are you doing up there?" Wyatt asked her.

"I'm terrible afraid of rats. I can deal with a little

mouse, but a rat is a different thing. It will attack when it's cornered, so I'll just sit right here until you take care of it. There wasn't no way I was going to let that critter get next to little Ella, no sir. Now, you go on into the kitchen and get the broom, or send Miss Bridget to get the gun and shoot the thing, but I'm not getting down from here until it's dead."

Bridget used a chair to crawl up onto the desk with Allie Mae. "Ella do all right?"

"Precious little doll slept the whole time you was gone."

"You've been sitting there for more than an hour?" Wyatt asked.

Allie Mae raised her chin a notch. "And I'd sit here until the rapture or I starved plumb to death before I'd get down and let that rat have a go at me."

Wyatt bit his lower lip to keep from laughing. The story got better every minute, and he could already hear Clayton laughing when he told it. "And this big, mean varmint is where?"

"He's under that settee." Allie Mae pointed.

Wyatt propped the front door open with the coatrack standing beside it and tiptoed toward the settee, where the monster was probably shaking in its hide beneath it. When he was directly behind the sofa, he commenced doing a stomp dance in his cowboy boots, the racket enough to scare the rat out of its hidey-hole and toward the open door. It was barely a flash of gray as it darted outside.

"If that wasn't the damnedest fool thing I've ever seen!" Bridget yelled.

Allie Mae nodded.

Ella set up a howl at being awakened so rudely.

Wyatt slid the coatrack back to its proper place and shut the door. "It's gone, isn't it? I've done my job. I got rid of it."

"No, I hired you to kill the thing. Now it'll find its way back into the kitchen and scare the bejesus out of us again."

Wyatt's whole face creased when he grinned. "Guess I don't get the job then, do I?"

"Oh, you get the job all right. You have to work for me now because you have to finish what you were hired to do. If the rat comes back, you will kill it. Come on, Allie Mae. We've got chores to do. It's only two hours until the customers start arriving. I expect Mr. Wyatt Ferguson can be back here with his baggage by then?" She shot him a look meant to drop his sorry old Texan carcass to the floor.

He kept smiling.

Bridget slung her legs over the side of the desk and attempted to stand, but one foot missed the chair.

Wyatt barely made it across the room in time to catch her when she fell. "Does my job include saving maidens from breaking their bones?" He used humor to cover the embarrassment of holding a perfect stranger as if he were about to carry her over to their marriage bedroom.

She wiggled. "Put me down right now."

He did. "You didn't answer my question."

Bridget propped her hands on her hips. "Your job involves helping run this hotel. If that means keeping me alive, then yes. If I say kill a rat, I don't mean to turn it loose so it can come back. If I tell you to wash dishes, then you do that."

Wyatt ignored the tirade and turned to help Allie Mae. "Give me your baby so you don't fall on your face too."

She handed him the wide-eyed, screaming child. "Ella ain't my baby."

"She's mine. Give her here," Bridget said.

"Where's your husband?"

"If I had a husband, do you think I'd be hiring you?"

"Killed in the war?"

"No, and that's enough. My private life is not a bit of your business. You going to take this job or not?" she asked. She soothed Ella with pats on the back and soft words. The baby quieted down and looked at the big man with round, cautious eyes.

"I think I just might," Wyatt answered. He'd never been one to sleep late, sit around and do nothing, and if he took this crazy job, he wouldn't have to go home to all the festivities. This little sawmill-town hotel offered room and board, plus temporary diversion from wheeling and dealing with the big oil companies, cattlemen, and Texas ranchers.

"Good. Go get your baggage, and pick out a room upstairs. We don't have any guests right now, so it's your choice. Come on, Allie Mae, let's go make pies."

With a brief nod, Wyatt walked out the door. He had half an hour to decide whether he'd really bring his trunk back to the Black Swan. That's how long it would take him to get to the station.

Chapter Two

Bridget had grown up in the Black Swan and knew every creak and sound whether by door, by floorboard, or by step. The front door groaned just slightly when opened. The floor in the lobby had a board close to the clerk's counter that sounded like a chirping bird. The fourth step on the staircase leading up to the guests' rooms told the tale when a boarder tried to sneak in late without making a sound.

So at the same time Wyatt Ferguson carried his trunk in from the porch, Bridget realized that something wasn't right. Amid the noise of the dinner crowd was a strange phenomenon, and that was a sudden quietness under her feet in the kitchen. Always there was a slight hum under her feet, coming from the generator. The strange piece of machinery that her father, Patrick, had installed to run the expensive refrigerator in their kitchen was in the basement, and it had stopped. Her mother had put up quite a fuss about spending their money on such a gadget when an icebox had worked fine their whole married life. The iceman still brought ice, didn't he? And not once had they poisoned anyone in the restaurant with spoiled meat or milk.

But nothing doing but Patrick O'Shea would have one of the newfangled refrigerators for the Black Swan, and he had paid more for it than he had their automobile. And the thing ran on a foreign chunk of machinery that Patrick said ran the motor that kept the refrigerator cold without the services of the iceman. Right in the middle of Bridget's serving the noon meal, the vibration stopped.

She met Wyatt in the lobby. "What do you know about refrigerators as opposed to iceboxes, Mr. Ferguson?"

"My name is Wyatt, and I know very little about them. Is this a test of some kind? Did I fail a second time, and you're going to send me and this danged heavy trunk back to the train station?"

"It is not a test, and how did you get that trunk here in the first place?" She crossed her arms over her chest and tapped her foot on the floor impatiently.

"I paid a man with a horse and buggy to drive me and it back here," he said.

Her eyebrows raised a notch. "You have money?"

"That's none of your business, Miz O'Shea. I agreed to work for you for a dollar a day and room and board. What I have or do not have is my business," he said.

"Fair enough. Your first job after you get that thing up to one of the rooms, is to go down to the basement through the door at the back of the stairs and see if you can do anything about the generator. Something is wrong. It quit humming." She began to have doubts about whether she'd picked the right man. Even though his feet were big enough to kill a rat, on second scrutiny he didn't have the lean, hungry look about him that most of the men who got off the train had. Good Lord, what if he was another one of those reporters or even an undercover detective still looking to find Ralph Contiello?

Without a word Wyatt hefted his trunk up to his shoulders and hauled it up to the landing, where he dropped it with a thud. Which room would he choose? Judging by all the open doors, the place didn't look as if it was overrun by guests. He saw four chambers on each side with a bathroom at the end. At least he could have a real bath after a hard day's work and not have to rely on a basin of water. He peeped into each room, finding them identical except for location. Good, sturdy oak furniture. A bed, washstand, dresser with a mirror, and a rocking chair. Crisp, clean curtains. Fresh smell. He'd stayed in a lot worse in his travels.

"What the devil am I doing?" he mumbled as he set the trunk inside the first door on the left right off the stairs.

By the time he opened the trunk and dragged out his faded work overalls and a chambray shirt with patches on the sleeves, he admitted why he'd delayed his trip back to Texas. It was Ilene, plain and simple. He couldn't have her, couldn't even attempt to have her. And yet he couldn't get the image of her just before he'd left out of his head. She'd been sitting on her second-floor balcony, brushing her long black silky hair. By the light of a full moon he'd seen her plainly from the grove of pecan trees where the shadows hid him. Just looking at her from afar had heated his blood to the boiling point, and he could do absolutely nothing about it.

He shucked off his clothing and laid it neatly on the bed, redressed in the worn overalls and shirt, and jerked on a pair of scuffed boots. He could hear voices out past the dining area when he reached the bottom of the stairs. The rat must have decided that outside was better than inside if it had to deal with those two women. The light from the basement doorway sliced through the darkness, and he saw a thread spool dangling from a string attached to the ceiling. When he jerked on it, a single bulb illuminated the basement. Not really enough to chase all the shadows from the corners but at least enough light to find the generator and motor. They were both much, much smaller than the ones on the oil rigs but worked on the same principle. It didn't look as if either had been maintained or cleaned in at least a year, so he set about the task methodically, the way he did everything. One thing at a time—carefully disassemble, clean, reassemble—thinking only about what he was doing and nothing else.

In an hour the motor and the generator both hummed into life. Wyatt sat down in an old kitchen chair and took stock of the whole area. That there was a basement at all in a building in southern Arkansas was strange. Flooring covered about half the room, a job started but left unfinished. Odds and ends of old furniture were strewn about, along with several trunks, no doubt filled with mementos and family things. What he was looking at was usually relegated to attics in that part of the country as well as in north central Texas, where he had grown up.

"Hey, I heard the noise. So you got it fixed?" Bridget called from the top of the stairs as she descended. She was amazed at the man sitting on the chair, truly seeing him for the first time as a man and not a potential rat killer. He had wavy blond hair that lay on his collar and needed a trip to the barber. His pale green eyes shot with golden flecks were beneath light brown brows, and a dimple on the left side of his angular face looked as if it would deepen if he smiled. His mouth was off kilter, the bottom lip fuller than the top one.

"It's fixed, boss lady. Want me to finish this floor?"

"Yes, I do. Starting today. The keys to the automobile are in cubbyhole number one behind the clerk's desk. Take the car and go to the lumberyard. Tell them I said to put whatever you need on the Black Swan bill," she said.

"You let me walk all the way back to the train station

and carry a trunk back here when you own an automobile?" he said testily.

"I don't drive. I hate the thing, so I forget it's there. Ira used it when he was here. Besides, you didn't carry a trunk back here. You hired a man to bring it for you," she said.

"Ira?"

"Catherine's fiancé and Alice's husband," Bridget said.

His eyebrows knit into a solid line.

Bridget folded her arms across her chest. "Catherine is my older sister. She's the earth, and she was engaged to Ira Newell, only he went off to war and died. Then Ira wasn't dead anymore, and he came back to Huttig, and Alice, the middle sister, who had been in love with him forever but didn't tell anyone—she's named for air—married him. He lived here and was our handyman until a couple of months ago, and he used the car. You are welcome to it anytime you need the thing. Like I said, I hate to drive."

Too much information in too few words swirled around in Wyatt's head, but not much of it made sense. So Bridget O'Shea was the youngest of three sisters who evidently owned the hotel together, and now the older two had married and moved away. That would be the reason she needed hired help, but earth and air?

"My name, Bridget, is for water in the Gaelic. And yes, I want this basement finished, so unless I call you to do something else, that's your next job."

"Do I get to eat first?" he asked.

"That's a stupid question, Mr. Ferguson. Of course you can eat first. The dining room and kitchen are always open to you. Come on up and help yourself. Breakfast is normally just me and Allie Mae, but I've always enjoyed a big meal at the start of the day, so it's served at seven. Dinner is the noon meal, and folks start coming in at about eleven-thirty. We try to shut it down at two. Then supper starts at four-thirty, and we close up shop at around seven."

"What's for dinner?"

"This is Monday. We have ham, candied yams, hot rolls, and desserts on Monday," she said as she started back up the stairs.

"That's it? Just one thing?" he asked.

"Take it or go hungry. I'm a dang fine cook, and our restaurant makes a good living even when the rooms aren't full," she said icily. Wasn't that just like a blasted man? Never satisfied with what he had and always looking for a reason to get mad about something. It was the very reason she'd never let one back into her heart.

"I'll be up shortly," he said.

She didn't even answer.

Wyatt didn't need a snippy woman in his life. He didn't have to stay in Huttig, Arkansas, while he waited for the next few weeks to pass. He could leave anytime he wanted. He'd signed no contracts, and grief was the very thing he didn't need. He made it to the lobby, and he heard a dining room full of people talking and enjoying their food while the smell of baked ham and chocolate cake wafted out to his nose. His stomach growled. He'd earned his dinner by fixing the generator, not to mention getting rid of the rat.

He went up to the bathroom and washed his hands, brushed his hair, and decided that the length of time it took to eat one meal and get back into his good clothing was how long he'd stay at the Black Swan. Nothing could make him tarry a minute longer. God knew he didn't need the money.

"Ilene," he moaned at his reflection in the mirror above the sink. If he wanted to be totally miserable, he could go home. If he wanted to be annoyed at Bridget O'Shea ninety percent of the time, he could stay. By the time he reached the dining room, he'd decided to stay and earn his angel wings. Bridget could aggravate the sin right out of a man.

Wyatt didn't know if he should go to the kitchen and eat in there, since he was hired help, or if he was free to sit at any table and be waited on. He'd never in his entire twenty-six years worked at a job other than for his own family. This new dollar-a-day world was an uncomfortable place, especially when a man was starving. He stood just inside the door until Bridget motioned him inside to a table in a far back corner.

"Sit here, and I'll bring you a plate as soon as I can," she said.

It annoyed him that she had the control. Other than his mother, who'd had to rule five sons, he'd never taken orders from a woman. He wasn't so sure he could endure it for six weeks. However, if he survived, he could go home after the wedding was over and done with, and that would definitely put Ilene out of his reach and, with luck, out of his mind.

Several café patrons eyed him as they ate, and he could feel the questions in their eyes. Who was this man Miss O'Shea had hired? Was he trustworthy? Why would she hire someone from outside the community?

Well, they could dang well answer their own questions, because he had plenty of them too. Beginning with, was Bridget a Miss or a Mrs.? If she were a Miss, where had that baby come from? And why were folks still giving her their business? In a small town like this, she likely would have been ostracized for having a child out of wedlock. And if it was Mrs., where was her husband? She'd said she didn't have one. Said he wasn't one of the many who'd fallen in the war. Maybe the flu had claimed him. One thing for sure, there wasn't a husband in attendance, or she wouldn't have hired him as the resident handyman.

A man with more wrinkles than a dried-up creek bed crossed the room and pulled out the chair across from him. "I'm Major Engram. Been livin' here since someone squatted under a pecan tree and Huttig sprung up around me. And who are you?"

"Wyatt Ferguson. I've been hired to take care of anything broken and kill any rats that venture into the Black Swan," he answered.

Bridget set a heaping plate of ham, sweet potatoes, baked beans, and hot rolls in front of him. "That's right. *Kill* the rat. Not turn him loose out the front door. You want your pie brought to this table, Major?"

"That would be fine. I'm just gettin' to know your new help here. Seein' if maybe he's a fisherman." The major winked.

"I'm a fisherman, all right," Wyatt said. "Got any creeks or ponds 'round close?"

"River ain't too far distant. We catch some good catfish and bass when they're runnin'—enough to fill our bellies sometimes. Son, you ain't got the looks of a hungry man. What brings you to Huttig?"

Wyatt stared at Major. Was this man kin to Bridget, and what business was it of his why Wyatt was in Huttig?

"It's like this," Major offered when Wyatt didn't answer. "Bridget's father was my friend. He was a flu victim, and so was her mother not quite a year ago. There are three girls—Catherine, Alice, and Bridget, with Bridget being the youngest and the most scatterbrained. Catherine could run this place without blinking an eye. But she up and left, and by the time she was gone, her fiancé, Ira Newell, came back into the picture to help out, and he ended up marryin' Alice. Now there's just Bridget, and I'm wanting to make sure you're not here for any shenanigans."

"I'm not," Wyatt said. He dug into the plate of food and almost swooned with delight. The ham was smoked to perfection and cooked long and slow, with a hint of blackberry wine to it, just like his mother made. The sweet potatoes had a fine crust of brown sugar and pecans over the top, and the hot rolls were flaky. He could put up with a scatterbrained woman easily for food like that.

"Then why are you here? You don't look like a soldier lookin' for work to me," Major said.

"I wasn't. I was just sitting in the station, and Miz O'Shea sat down beside me and said I'd do fine. She looked at my feet first. I think she was looking for someone to kill a rat," he said between bites.

Major chuckled. "That's Bridget. Her mind don't work like other folks'. Not as bad as Alice always let on to be, but her momma named her right. Said Bridget was named for water, and a person couldn't live without it, but it was unstable, and that's our Bridget. She's just now gettin' over that ordeal last year and speakin' her own mind, tryin' to step up and run a hotel without Catherine to guide her. I'm just makin' sure you ain't here to hoodwink her."

"Rest assured, Mr. Major, I'm here for a six-week job, and then I'm leaving this area. Wild horses couldn't keep me in this place longer than that," he said.

"Fair enough. You've got your reasons. I've stated mine. We're on even ground now. We'll have to go to the river some evening and catch a few fish," Major said.

"That would be nice," Wyatt said.

Bridget set a healthy chunk of meringue-topped coconut cream pie in front of Major and edged another close to Wyatt's plate. "I brought your pie with Major's since I was headed this way. If you want seconds, there's plenty in the kitchen."

"Thanks." Wyatt nodded.

The next time Bridget came out of the kitchen, she had the baby on one hip and a tea pitcher in the other hand, replenishing empty glasses. Wyatt watched from the corner of his eye as he finished his ham and dove right into the pie. It was every bit as good as his mother's, and he would definitely be raiding the kitchen for another chunk before suppertime.

"She's a good woman. Might grow up to be a great one now that she has to stand on her own two feet," Major said. "You got a mind for a good woman?"

"No sir!" Wyatt almost choked on cream pie.

"Seein' as how you have a job and you're not too blasted ugly, I reckon there'll be those who's goin' to start right away tryin' to hitch you up with one of the eligible girls around here. You'd better get ready to run or get caught," Major said.

Wyatt grinned. "I've been a fast runner most of my grown life." What he'd give to get caught by Ilene, though, couldn't be measured in dollars and cents. The one woman in the whole state of Texas he'd let outrun him, and she was already spoken for.

Bridget passed Mabel's table and stopped to pour tea. "Ya'll think it's going to snow?" she asked.

"Snow in these parts? Girl, how many times you seen

snow around Huttig?" Mabel asked. "And who's that man over there with Major?"

Bridget set the pitcher in the middle of the table and readjusted Ella's weight on her hip. "My new hired hand. He's going to finish the basement floor and do any other odd jobs I can find for him."

"You aren't going to let him live here, are you?" Mabel whispered as if she were tattling a major sin to St. Peter.

"Same deal as we had with Ira. Room and board and a dollar a day. That's the going rate for good help, I suppose," Bridget said.

"Your mother would turn over in her grave if she knew how you girls have behaved since her death. Ira was a trusted family friend. This man is a stranger. You got into bad trouble with a stranger before. What's it going to take to put sense into that head of yours?" Acid fairly dripped from Mabel's tongue.

"Momma would applaud us all for standing on our own two feet and making decisions that bring us happiness." Bridget smiled brightly, her aqua eyes dancing at the vision of her mother doing such a thing even if she were able. "If you will excuse me, I've got to make the rounds one more time."

"That baby needs a father," Mabel said.

"This baby has all she needs in me." Bridget's smile faded quickly.

"What's his name?"

"It's a girl, and her name is Ella, just like my momma. And you've known that since the day she was born," Bridget said. Good grief, Mabel lived right next door and was in and out of the hotel dining room with her two friends several times a week. Had the woman gone daft?

"Not your child, Bridget. That man you've hired. What's his name?"

"Mr. Ferguson. Wyatt Ferguson."

"Where did you find him?"

"At the train station. I decided that, come hell or high water, I was going to hire some help, and I did."

"You're going to let a hobo live in the Black Swan? Why, girl, he's liable to kill you in your sleep and rob you blind. Besides, a proper lady doesn't say things like 'hell or high water,'" Mabel declared.

"He's not a hobo, and it's really none of your business, and, darlin', you just said 'hell' yourself. I trust you'll spend some time on your knees begging for forgiveness," Bridget said as she moved away from the table. But the doubt had been planted. What had she done in a moment of anger at a stupid rat? Gone out and hired someone who might hurt Ella?

She made her way back to the kitchen, where she and Allie Mae cleaned up the dishes and prepared for the supper crowd. Allie Mae rolled pie dough to make a few more pies, since one small slice was all that was left of the half dozen they'd prepared that morning.

"I'm going to take Ella into the back room, feed her,

and get her ready for a nap," Bridget said when she'd finished drying dishes.

"He's a good-lookin' one, that feller you hired. Wish I was a little older." Allie Mae blushed.

"Good-lookin' men are worse than ugly ones. Remember that, and choose wisely," Bridget said seriously.

"Was your husband good-lookin'?"

"He was very handsome—and very mean."

"Don't mean all men that's easy on the eyes would be like your husband, does it?" Allie Mae asked.

"No, it doesn't. I'm just saying that you get to know a man for a long time before you up and marry him. Know his momma and his daddy and all his brothers and sisters, and make him really mad a few times to see what happens when he's upset," Bridget said.

"Like Orville?" Allie Mae blushed again.

"That's right. Like Orville. You've grown up with him. You know what he's like."

"Guess you are right, but that one you hired is almighty pretty," Allie Mae said. "Course, he's an old man. I bet he's pushin' thirty."

Bridget patted Allie Mae on the shoulder and left her to the pie dough. She found Wyatt writing figures on a piece of paper he'd found behind the clerk's desk.

"I'm figuring the amount of feet you need for the basement floor job," he explained.

"Let's get something straight before we go any further," she said.

He looked up.

"Are you the type to hurt me in any way? Or my baby daughter?"

"No, ma'am, I would never hurt a woman or a child. I'm just here to work a few weeks, then I'll be going on home to Texas," he said.

"Why'd you stop anyway? If you got family in Texas, why aren't you there?"

"I'm on my way, but I could use a job for about six weeks. I figure that'd be somewhere up around forty-two dollars." He did the arithmetic in his head. So little for so much, but it would be good hard work and would keep his mind off of things, people, and places it had no business thinking on.

"Fair enough. I'm not as steady on my feet as Catherine always was, but I've learned the hard way how to read people. I didn't picture you as an evil man, but I wanted to ask and be sure. When you get that job done in the basement, I'd like you to check the attic. While it's cool enough to get up there, I'd like to have it finished also. It's going to get hot before long, and no one could work up there in the summer heat. Tonight after supper it will be your job to take the money from the paying customers and tally up the amounts for those who charge by the month. You any good at figuring like that?"

"I reckon I can do it without too many mistakes," he said, an edge to his voice.

"Good. That's your job after dinner and supper from now on. In between times you can take care of the handyman stuff."

"Yes, ma'am," he said.

"You got a problem with me, Mr. Ferguson?" She eyed him carefully, not liking his cold tone.

"No, ma'am, I do not," he said.

"You're lying, but I expect you've got your reasons not to trust a woman just like I've got mine about trusting menfolk. I'll stay out of your way and not bruise your pride as much as possible."

His jaw worked in anger. "It would take more than something your size to bruise my pride."

"Don't judge a book by its cover. It might surprise the hell out of you," she said.

She sounded so much like his mother, down to using profanity, that he was stunned.

Chapter Three

When Bridget awoke on Wednesday morning, two inches of wet snow covered the ground, and it was still falling, sticking to the tree limbs and pine needles like bits of icing on a cake. The sky was pale gray, and everything was eerily quiet. Most mornings a bird of some kind could be heard welcoming a new day. She tucked the covers around Ella a little tighter and dressed in black and white checked overalls and a long-sleeved blouse, white with a round collar and tight-fitting cuffs.

She was in the lobby heading for the basement door when Wyatt opened it and startled her. It had only been two days since she hired him, and in her stunned amazement at snow she'd forgotten that he was in the hotel.

"Fire is started and booming. I pulled some rugs over the vents into the seven rooms not being used upstairs and closed the doors. No use heating what's not being used. I did leave the bathroom door open for fear the pipes might freeze, although it looks like your father wrapped them well."

"Thank you. From now on the fire can be your job," she said, thankful to have someone go down to the basement every morning. She hated that place and always imagined mice hiding in the corners ready to run out and scare the devil out of her.

"I can do that, ma'am," he said. "Allie Mae need a ride to work? I could drive to town and get her."

"No, I'm going to make a phone call and tell her we're closing today. No one will come out in this kind of weather."

"Phone call?" Wyatt raised an eyebrow. Telephones were for the eccentric and very rich. A simple little hotel like the Black Swan shouldn't even have a refrigerator, much less a telephone.

"Yes, Papa did like his gadgets. We never fussed about the indoor plumbing. But Momma was put out over the refrigerator. She said that it would take ten years worth of ice to pay for the thing. And she never could see the use of having a telephone in the hotel. It hasn't been used more than thirty times since it's been sitting under the clerk's counter, but I'm using it today," she said.

"Allie Mae has a telephone in her home, and she works here?" He was truly puzzled. He assumed the girl was poor; she wore ill-fitting clothing and, well, just looked as if she couldn't afford better.

"No, silly. Allie Mae lives a few houses away from the Commercial. I'll call Buddy, the night clerk who's on duty until seven. He'll catch her when she walks past and send her on back home."

"Commercial?"

"That would be the big company hotel. It was built after the Black Swan and gets most of the business from the mill. The mill owns the hotel and the store," she explained.

"The white hotel with the wraparound balcony and porch?" he asked.

"That's right. Probably where you were hoping to stay if you'd found a job at the mill, right?" she said as she made her way across the cold floor to the clerk's desk. She pulled a phone out, had the operator ring up the Commercial hotel, and told Buddy to give Allie Mae the message.

"That won't be necessary. Just catch her on the way. If you're sure it's no bother. Tell Orville thank you," Bridget said.

"Orville?" Wyatt asked.

"Orville is sweet on Allie Mae. He works at the Commercial. He's going to walk over to her house and give her the message."

"Allie Mae isn't old enough to have a boyfriend," he said.

"You are not her father, Wyatt Ferguson. She'll be sixteen in the spring. Women get married at that age in this part of the world."

"Did you?"

"Did you?" she countered.

"I'm not married and never have been," Wyatt said.

"Well, I was married and never intend to be again," she said.

"Do I have time to haul lumber from the front porch to the basement before breakfast?" He changed the subject.

"I would say you've got half an hour. It won't take long to stir up breakfast for two," she said. So he'd never been married. Let Mabel hear that something as handsome as Wyatt had landed in Huttig, didn't have a wife, and hadn't had one in the past. No divorce to taint him. No fiancée to mark him. He was fair play, and Mabel was a bona fide matchmaker as well as Union County's best gossip. He might be taking more than a trunk back to Texas with him in six weeks.

Wyatt wondered what lay beyond the door leading into Bridget O'Shea's private quarters as he slipped into his coat, which had been hanging on the coatrack behind the front door. Not that he was interested in the woman. No sir. She was the exact opposite of Ilene, the woman who haunted his dreams and was keeping him away from Alvord until spring. Curiosity had always been his downfall. It's what put him into the job that he held for his family's company. What was out there? What could he uncover? What could he talk people into letting him buy?

It was the same with Ilene. What would it be like to

kiss her? How would it feel if he brushed that long, black hair for her? Would he make a good husband if she consented to marry him instead of . . . ? He shook the crazy notions from his head and dug a pair of gloves from his coat pocket.

He opened the door to a bitter blast of cold air and a snowball hurling through the air caught him right between the eyes. For a moment he was stunned, not from the pain but from the sudden impact so early in the morning. It reminded him of the few times it had snowed in Alvord and his brother, Clayton, arose before he did to make a mountain of snowballs. By the time Wyatt went outside, Clayton had an arsenal ready for battle, and Wyatt had to form and throw with speed to keep up with him.

A small boy of about six or seven ran up to the edge of the porch. "I'm right sorry, mister. I was throwin' at Joe Bill, and he dodged, and it hit you."

"No harm done," Wyatt said. "Who is Joe Bill?"

"He's my friend from next door. We was hopin' it would snow so we could have a real fight and build a snowman. We ain't seen much snow, and we don't even have to go to school, and who are you?"

"I'm Wyatt Ferguson."

"You goin' to marry up with Miss Bridget?"

"Hell, no!"

"That's a bad word. Momma says if I say a bad word, she'll tan my hide. Joe Bill says bad words, but his momma don't care."

Wyatt noticed that the child's hands were scarlet and gloveless. He pulled his own gloves off and pushed them toward the boy. "Here, you take these. Your fingers are going to fall off."

"Can't. Momma says we don't take no charity."

"Then I'll sell them to you for a dime. You can help me take this board into the house and down the steps to the basement, and I'll pay you a dime so you can buy them. What's your name?"

"Name is Clark, and I ain't goin' in that hotel, not even for a dime or them fancy gloves."

"Why, Clark?" Wyatt asked.

" 'Cause that place is hainted."

"Oh? This hotel is haunted? How do you figure that?" Wyatt kept the smile from his face, but it wasn't easy. The child looked so serious.

A snowball came from around the corner of the house next door and landed two feet from Clark. He swept it up and gave it a heave, hitting the other boy on the run.

"You've got a good arm there, son. You going to play baseball?" Wyatt asked.

"Someday I am. I'm goin' to go to war and fight first, and then I'm goin' to come home and play baseball. That kind where they give you money," he said.

"Sure you don't want to help me move this board before you do all that? I could use the help," Wyatt said.

"No sir. That place is hainted. It's got Miss Bridget's

mean old husband's ghost in there. They killed him, you know."

"Who killed him?" Wyatt's curiosity was piqued. Snow collected on his hair, his nose was frozen, and yet the hair on his neck stood up as if there was an electrical storm in progress rather than a winter snowstorm.

"They did. Miss Catherine and Miss Alice and Miss Bridget. He come here and left, but then he come back, and they killed him. One man come and digged everywhere, but he didn't dig up her husband because he's still in that house. He's a ghost, and it's hainted, and I'm not ever goin' in there. I'm afraid of that man. He was mean."

"I see. Well, I've got to go to work now, Clark. Maybe we'll talk another time when I'm outside," Wyatt said.

"We can talk any old time but not in there. Me and Joe Bill, we saw him when he come to beat up Miss Bridget. If we'd had us a gun, we might've kilt him ourselves for bein' so mean."

A snowball came through the air and caught Clark on the arm. He raced off to take care of the more important business. Wyatt just hoped he didn't get frostbite on his young, tender fingers.

He maneuvered two long flooring planks down to the basement before Bridget called him to breakfast. She'd made sausage and scrambled eggs, light and fluffy, and a pan of biscuits. They served themselves from the stove and ate at the worktable in the kitchen with Ella in her mother's arms.

Wyatt had had the better part of half an hour to think about what he'd heard from the boy next door, and he had a thousand questions he wanted to ask Bridget, but he didn't figure she'd answer the first one, much less all of them. Most likely she'd fire him on the spot. It was snowing, and he didn't feel like toting his chest a mile back to the rail station, so he kept his mouth shut.

"I heard you talking to Clark from next door," she said.

The hair on his neck prickled again, and he nodded, grateful for a mouthful of eggs so he couldn't talk without thinking first.

"He's a nice boy as far as boys go. His folks, Lizzy and Roy, are good neighbors. Lizzy's sister used to work for me and Alice, back last fall," she said.

"I asked him if he wanted to make a dime and help me carry the floor planks inside," Wyatt said.

"And?" Bridget asked.

"He was too busy playing," Wyatt told her.

"He's probably tickled for a day out of school," Bridget said. She was glad for Wyatt's company and wished they had more in common to talk about. She missed her sisters terribly, but they were both happy in their marriages—something she'd never been—and for that she was thankful.

"Why do you run this business all alone?" Wyatt asked.

"I don't. I have Allie Mae and you to help me. Besides, Momma and Papa ran it, just the two of them, and did very well all those years until we three girls were old enough to help, so it's not an impossible feat, just a boring one at times."

The silence between them after that comment wasn't uncomfortable, just boring, as she'd said. Wyatt finished eating, told her the meal was good, and went on about his work in the basement.

Bridget laid Ella in a cradle in the kitchen and set about washing the dishes and boiling stew meat for dinner and supper. A nice pot of soup would stick to Wyatt's ribs and keep him warm. She'd make an apple nut cake for dessert. When the hotel and restaurant were open for business, the fare was unvarying. Monday, baked ham. Tuesday, pot roast. Wednesday, chicken and dumplings. Et cetera. It would be nice to prepare something that hadn't been carved in stone from the day the Black Swan opened.

Wyatt was on his way to the porch for another plank when Mabel pushed her way inside. He stepped back and allowed her access to the lobby. He'd seen the woman in the dining room the first day he was there and several times out around the house on the west side of the hotel. Clark lived on the eastern side, Mabel and her husband on the other. Both were shotgun-styled mill houses, but it was evident Mabel's husband had done some additions and kept up the repairs better than Clark's family.

"Where is Bridget?" she asked icily.

"In the kitchen, I would suppose," Wyatt answered.

"Why would a decent man like you be living here in this hotel? You should be out looking for a job."

"Why? I have a job. It pays well, and the food and accommodations are very good," he said.

Mabel snorted. "Watch your step and your tone, young man. You never know when you might disappear into the night like her husband did. They haven't found his body yet. Might not ever find yours either."

Wyatt leaned against the banister and made a mental note to tighten up the newel post. "And why would her husband disappear?"

"Oh, he was an evil one, he was, but that doesn't give those O'Shea girls the right to kill him and get away with it—no sir, it does not. Bible is definite on that. Body kills, body pays. They ain't paid yet," Mabel whispered.

"Why would they kill him?"

"He beat her awful bad. Mean as a snake, that Ralph Contiello was, but that don't give her the right to kill him. You just watch your step and keep your eyes open. You might find another job if you ask around," Mabel whispered.

Bridget poked her head around the dining room archway. "Mabel, what brings you out in weather like this?"

"I'd like to buy a pie if you're cookin' today. Maybe coconut?"

"No, ma'am, I'm not baking pies today. Closed up until the snow stops and melts. No use in cooking up a bunch of food to go to waste. I'm making an apple cake for our dinner and supper because I've got a few apples about to go bad. You want me to put an extra one in the oven and bring it over when it's done?" Bridget asked.

"No, I've got cake in the house. Thanks anyway." Mabel gave Wyatt a knowing look and went back out into the gray day, leaving two wet footprints on the floor in front of the rug at the end of the staircase.

Bridget blanched when she looked at the rug, memories she'd tried so hard to bury for nearly a year flashing through her mind. She set her jaw and willed them away, then gave Wyatt a tight smile. "She's nosy but harmless."

"You think she didn't even want a pie?" Wyatt asked.

"She's going to fish out information about you and then set about finding a nice local girl to entice you with. There's lots more women than men since the war, and Mabel is a matchmaker as well as a world-renowned gossip. Beware if you aren't thinkin' on takin' a wife home to Texas with you. She tried to rope poor old Ira into marrying her niece," Bridget said.

"Your brother-in-law Ira?" Wyatt asked, and he saw a huge black spider on the doorjamb not a foot behind Bridget's nodding head.

He raised a fist, took two hurried steps toward her, and reached over her shoulder to smash the bug. She dropped to the floor, rolled up into a fetal position, and began to tremble.

Wyatt knelt beside her and touched her shoulder.

She flinched.

He withdrew his hand immediately. "Bridget, it was a spider. I'm not going to hit you. I'm sorry I scared you. I was just killing a spider."

"Don't ever raise your fist at me again or I will fire you," she said in a hollow voice as she uncurled and sat up.

"I did not raise my fist at you to begin with. I was killing a spider on the wall behind you. If you'll look, it's lying on the floor right there," he said defensively.

She glanced down, and the sight of the hairy dead spider didn't terrify her nearly as much as the fear of being hit again.

She tried to stand up, but her knees were still weak. "Tell me before you hit anything again so I can be prepared."

"Let me help you." Wyatt reached out.

"Don't touch me. Don't ever touch me. I don't . . . I can't . . . just keep your distance, Mr. Ferguson. I'm going back to the kitchen." Bridget's blue eyes still held fear.

She made her trembling knees carry her to the kitchen, where she slid down on the floor beside Ella's cradle. The baby slept soundly, and Bridget wept quietly.

Wyatt wondered the rest of the morning if he was covering up the remains of Ralph Contiello under the new floor of the basement. It would be the ideal place to hide a dead body, but Clark had told him a detective had dug up the whole place. Besides, there was no rotting smell in the basement. Bridget would have had to dug deep to keep down the odor, and she didn't look big enough or strong enough to do such a deed.

He hoped Ralph Contiello was dead. Any man who hit a woman and caused such fear as he'd seen in Bridget didn't deserve to live. However, Wyatt did spend the morning wondering just where three women would take a dead body, how they'd get it there, and what they'd do with it. The smartest thing would have been not to bury it at all but to weight it down and give it to the river Major Engram had mentioned. If that's what they did, it would be nothing more than a skeleton by now. Maybe some good-sized storms had created enough stir to push the bones all the way out to the Gulf of Mexico.

He hammered in a board and went back to the porch for another one. The skies had lightened, and the snow had stopped. A slash of blue and a small ray of sunshine shot through the winter gray. Bridget held the door open for him, but was very careful to move in such a way that he didn't touch her even accidentally.

"Mr. Ferguson, I feel I owe you an explanation," she said when she'd shut the door behind him. "If you will lay that board on the floor, I will explain."

He bent over and put the wood on the floor. "Miz O'Shea, I understand. You don't have to say anything."

"Oh, but I do. You see, there are rumors you are bound to hear, since you will work and live here for the next several weeks. I was married to Ralph Contiello, a very rich man from over in El Dorado. He was abusive and had forbidden me to come to my dying mother's bedside. I did anyway." Her voice was flat as she drew in enough breath to finish. "He followed me and intended to beat me again, but I shot at him with my mother's gun. Missed him. The bullet hole is still in the woodwork in room number two up there. He left that night and has never been heard from since. Rumor has it that my sisters and I killed him. We didn't, Mr. Ferguson. Rumor also has it that we buried him on the property. We didn't. You have nothing to fear from me. I won't shoot you in your sleep."

"And you have nothing to fear from me," he said. "I don't hit women."

"Not even when you are very, very angry?"

"Never."

Bridget simply nodded and kept her face blank on purpose. She didn't believe him. Probably the only man who'd never hit a woman in anger was her father. Patrick O'Shea had a temper of the worst kind, and politics could send him into two-hour discussions that got very, very loud. However, he would have never hit one of his womenfolk. She'd figured all men were like him. She'd been wrong. Ralph wasn't loud. He seldom yelled. He just found reasons to whip her and did it. She'd never live like that again, and she'd never trust another man.

"I'll get on back to work. Thank you for explaining," Wyatt said.

"You aren't going to quit working for me, then?"

"No, ma'am. I'm not real afraid that something as little as you is going to kill me in my sleep or bury me under the basement floorboards," he said.

She giggled, and her eyes glittered.

In that moment he saw the little girl Bridget had been at one time. For a brief moment a spark of merriment and happiness filled the room, but before it was fully born, it was gone.

Then the door flew open, and a force that had nothing to do with the weather blew into the room. Before Wyatt could tear his eyes from Bridget's, she let out a squeal and literally jumped a foot off the floor into the air. He expected her to fall into a heap again and shrivel up into a ball, but instead she was laughing and hugging a tall woman with the darkest auburn hair he'd ever seen. A man, equally tall, with dark hair and a business suit stood behind them.

"Catherine!" Bridget patted the woman on the back while she continued to hug her. "Why on earth are you two out in this kind of weather?"

The man looked across the room. "Wyatt Ferguson?"

"Quincy?" Wyatt's green eyes widened.

"You two know each other?" Bridget asked.

"We met once in a train station. Had to spend a while there, so we talked," Wyatt said quickly. "I'm working for Miz O'Shea. Dollar a day and room and board. Pretty good job, isn't it?"

Quincy heard the words but couldn't believe them, but evidently his old friend wanted to remain anonymous, so he wouldn't give away the secret. "Sounds like a deal to me. What are you doing on a day like this?"

"Finishing the basement floor," Wyatt said.

"I'll get Catherine settled and come down to visit

with you a spell while these sisters catch up on their gossip," Quincy said.

"I'll be there."

"Now tell me what you are doing here," Bridget said to Catherine.

"First, where is Ella? I can't wait to hold her. Has she grown much?"

Bridget led the way to the kitchen, where Ella had awakened from her nap. "It's only been a month since Christmas, but, yes, she's grown."

Catherine picked her up and held her close. "We're on our way to southern Louisiana on a very short job. Two weeks, maximum, and then over to Houston for a meeting. We decided to make it a road trip but didn't know how bad the roads were until we got to Strong. It was slippery from there down to here. Now it's your turn to talk. Who is that handsome new feller?"

"Wyatt Ferguson. I hired him to help," Bridget said.

"Good for you. This place is too much for you and Allie Mae."

"I miss you and Alice so much." Bridget sighed.

"But you are doing a fine job, and it's good for you, sister. You need the independence of it after what Ralph put you through," Catherine said.

"Do you think we'll ever forget that night?"

"No, but the memories will fade. Do you like Wyatt? How is he working out? Where is he from?"

"Alvord, Texas, and he's only here for six weeks, and then he's going home."

"Alvord?" Catherine mused. What the devil was a Ferguson from Alvord doing in Huttig, and how had Bridget talked him into working for her?

"That's what he said. Fact is, I was cornered by a rat." Bridget went on to tell the whole story about how she'd hired Wyatt because he had big feet.

Catherine laughed until tears rolled down her cheeks. The story was funny right then, but in six weeks when Catherine told her sister whom she'd hired to work for a dollar a day, it would be even funnier.

"Maybe while you're here you could take care of the El Dorado business?" Bridget said.

Catherine shook her head. "No. That's part of the job you've taken on. You can do it, Bridget. You are a strong woman."

"Today, I doubt that," Bridget whispered.

Chapter Four

Quincy sat on a kitchen chair with a broken back and watched Wyatt hammer nails into floorboards. "So tell me what the devil is going on here. You know this is one of two places I didn't dig up around here. By the time I knew there was even a basement under the house, I could trust Catherine to tell me the truth, and she said Ralph wasn't down here."

Both men stood at a few inches over six feet. Quincy had dark hair and eyes; Wyatt was blond with green eyes. Quincy wore a three-piece pinstriped suit and kid leather shoes. Wyatt wore bib overalls and a patched shirt. Nothing would have tagged them as coming from similar backgrounds.

Wyatt finished the last nail on that particular plank and braced his back against the wall to finish the story.

"The neighbor, Mabel, told me about good old Ralph Contiello. You were the one who came to investigate, weren't you?"

"I was. How did you wind up at the Black Swan?" Quincy asked.

"I was just passing through, waiting for the next train, when Bridget sat down beside me at the station."

"What are you running from?"

"A woman—what else?" Wyatt answered.

"Why?"

"She belongs to my best friend, and I don't trust myself to leave it that way. So you didn't even find a whiff of what happened to Ralph?"

Quincy shook his head. "I still think they did something with his body. I'm not sure how he died or who did the killing, and I'll never know. It's a sister secret they'll take to their grave, and I can live with that as long as I have Catherine," Quincy said.

"Are all the sisters red-haired?" Wyatt asked.

"They are. Catherine has the dark burgundy hair and the darkest green eyes. Alice was probably a carrottop as a child, but it's a little darker now, and her eyes are lighter green. Bridget is the strawberry blond with the pale aqua eyes. Each successive daughter got paler and shorter."

"Bridget's eyes look blue to me," Wyatt said.

"They change with the mood. So do Catherine's. When they go dark and wide, I know we're in for an argument." Quincy grinned.

"Don't tell Bridget about me, please," Wyatt said.

"Why would you not want her to know?"

"Because for the next few weeks I'd just as soon be plain old Wyatt Ferguson who's a handyman. At the end of six weeks I'll go home, and this will just be a moment in history that I'll forget all about."

"What do you think of Huttig?"

"It's the end of the world. If you take a step in the wrong direction, I'm afraid you'd fall off the edge into purgatory," Wyatt said.

"I felt the same way the few weeks I was here," Quincy said.

"And yet you come back?"

"It's Catherine's home, and Bridget is still here. It's not easy for her to let Bridget spread her wings and fly when she's been the keeper all these years," Quincy said.

"I thought their mother and father had only been dead a year or so."

"That's right, but Catherine is the earth." Quincy smiled.

"That's something I've heard before. What are you talking about?"

"Evidently their mother named them for the elements, and rightly so. Catherine for the earth, and she's stable and dependable. Alice for air, and she's, well, you'd have to meet her. She let people think she was slightly daft for years, but I saw through it pretty quick. However, it's not that she's dumb or even not bright. She's a freethinker and free as the air. Bridget was named for water. She's about that stable, but there's something about her that is eerie—as if she's looking through water with those big ocean-colored eyes straight into your soul."

"I think I understand, but it doesn't matter anyway. Bridget is my employer, and that's as far as it goes," Wyatt said.

"I remember saying something akin to that almost a year ago." Quincy grinned.

Wyatt shot him a dirty look and went back to work.

Bridget sighed deeply in contentment. Catherine's presence brought stability to the hotel. The universe was in the right place, and nothing could ever hurt Bridget when Catherine was home.

"So tell me more about Wyatt Ferguson. This is Wednesday. Is it traditional fare today, even though you're closed?" Catherine asked as they prepared dinner together. Quincy would love chicken and dumplings on a cold, wintry day, and chocolate cake was one of his favorite desserts.

"No, I'm making a good soup with stew meat and an apple nut cake. Something different. Besides, remember, I don't like chicken and dumplings, and since I didn't know you were coming, I already started the soup. And about Wyatt? I told you everything. He's a hired hand," Bridget said. "Tell me about you and Quincy. Why are you going to Louisiana? I thought he was in an office these days and you were both in Little Rock all the time."

"He gets antsy. He likes fieldwork, so we've agreed

that a couple of times a year we'll go out on a short job." Catherine shrugged.

"And you?"

"Got to admit, I love it all. I like being in my own home, and I adore Quincy. But I do enjoy the travel too, so this works fine. I'm starving. Shall I go holler for the menfolk?"

"I'll get a table set while they wash up. I'm just so glad you are here and that the weather is horrible. That way I have you all to myself for the day and don't have to share you with everyone who comes through the door," Bridget said.

"Me too." Catherine carried Ella with her as she went to call her husband and Bridget's handyman up for dinner.

It seemed strange to Bridget to sit in the dining room at a table for four with the rest of the room empty. Cozy but odd. She and Catherine took turns holding Ella while the other ate and the two men talked weather, the 1919 World Series, and the new Prohibition law. To Bridget's amazement, Wyatt kept up and voiced his opinion on every matter. How did a hobo get to be so knowledgeable on so many subjects? She scarcely had time to think the question, much less ponder over it, because Catherine came up with a preposterous idea about the time they started to cut the cake.

"Weather is bad but only in this area. I swear, if you can get past Strong, it's cold but clear. Folks aren't going to get out in the snow—or the mud when it starts to melt—so why don't you go on to El Dorado and take care of the banking this week? Wyatt could drive the Ford for you, so you and Ella would be more comfortable than on the train. Just hang a sign in the front window and tell everyone you are closed until the first of the week."

Bridget went as white as the snow. "I couldn't."

"I don't mind. My rate is a dollar a day whether I'm chauffeuring or putting a floor in the basement," Wyatt said.

Quincy covered a chuckle with his napkin. Catherine kicked his shin under the table.

Bridget looked at Catherine. "But where would we stay? Can we go and come back in one day? You always stay overnight."

"You'll stay at the hotel where I do. Use that telephone, and call them to make reservations. The number is in the business book. Tell them you want two rooms with an adjoining door," Catherine said.

"Is that proper?"

"It is if Wyatt is your bodyguard," Catherine said.

All the color went out of Bridget's face. "Why would I . . . oh, I see."

"A bodyguard should make a little more than a common laborer, shouldn't he?" Quincy asked.

That netted him a kick in the other shinbone.

"I'll work for the same amount, Miz O'Shea," Wyatt said. "It's no never-mind to me what I do."

"Do you really think it's the thing to do?" Bridget asked Catherine.

"You said you could run this place without me or Alice. That involves going to El Dorado every three months to make a deposit and sit down with the banker to find out how your accounts are. Then you have the banker send a check for twenty-five percent of the profits to Alice and put mine into the savings account right there in the bank," Catherine said.

"I suppose Alice is probably looking for her check. She and Ira might even need it for the spring planting," Bridget mused aloud.

Catherine smoothed the front of her emerald green velvet traveling suit. "I wouldn't be surprised."

"Okay, then, we'll do it. This is Wednesday. We'll go on Thursday, spend the night, and come back Friday," she said.

"Ah, why don't you take a few days? Have Wyatt drive you over to Crockett or maybe into Texarkana. Business is always slow this time of year anyway," Catherine said. "It'd do you good to get out and get away."

"Until Sunday, then?" Bridget said.

"Hang a sign on the door that says you'll be closed until further notice. That way you won't be obligated to come home on a particular day," Quincy said.

Wyatt eyed him skeptically. If he didn't know better, he'd think his old college friend was playing matchmaker, but surely Quincy wouldn't do such a fool thing. Not with Bridget O'Shea. Not that she wasn't a lovely woman, with all that thick, light red hair and those luminescent green eyes that were blue at times and, as Quincy said, turned darker when she was in deep thought. He simply wasn't interested in anyone right then. If he couldn't have Ilene, he'd be a self-proclaimed bachelor the rest of his life. His mother had four other sons to give her grandchildren and carry on the Ferguson name.

"It's a bit of a scary idea," Bridget said. "I'm very content right here in my own world. I don't need adventure."

Catherine's deep olive green eyes glittered. "Like me?"

"Or like Alice," Bridget said.

"It will be good for you. Four times a year you will go to El Dorado. After the first time you'll be looking forward to getting away, where someone else cooks for you and the stores offer more than Minnie and Tommy do down at the general store," Catherine said.

"I do miss the shopping in El Dorado," Bridget admitted.

Catherine polished off the last of the cake on her plate and cut another piece, making sure she got a corner with lots of icing. "So it's a deal?"

"Yes, it is," Bridget said, but it took every bit of her courage to say it without faltering.

The next morning dawned bright and beautiful with a winter sky of pale blue dotted with only a few puffs of scattered clouds. The snow had begun to melt with the arrival of a bright, warm sun, and what had been a beautiful white coverlet quickly turned into muddy, soggy earth. Catherine and Quincy departed right after breakfast, leaving behind a nervous Bridget.

"Okay, I've drained the pipes and made sure the fire is cold in the furnace. What else needs to be done?" Wyatt asked.

Bridget wrung the handkerchief in her hands. "I have no idea. I've never done this before, and I'm not sure it's a wise idea even now. Catherine talked me into it. I'm not sure I can even go into El Dorado with the Contiellos still there or that I'm ready to face the place again."

"Your sister's arguments made sense to me. You need to know how to do the banking end of things, and you've not been away from Huttig in nearly a year. I can drive the car, and you won't have to ride the train with Ella. Why is that such an ordeal?" Wyatt asked. He wore his three-piece suit and overcoat, his bags were packed for an overnight trip, and his hat was in his hands.

"Then load it all into the car, and we'll go before I really lose my nerve," she said.

Thirty minutes later Wyatt backed the Ford out into the road and turned toward Strong, Arkansas, a small town eleven miles from Huttig. The roads were muddy and potholed, but that's what they'd have all the way into El Dorado. Things were about to change in El Dorado, and Wyatt knew it because he'd implemented the groundwork for the changes that would blow the town's seams apart by spring. But on that cold January day things were still the same, and Bridget would have a trip into the El Dorado that she'd known in her married life. After that she'd be on her own and could battle the crowds that would be brought on by the oil boom.

It wasn't a perhaps or even a maybe. Wyatt had been instrumental in the first round of buying and selling, and the drillers were already on the way to southern Arkansas to dip into the reserves he knew lay beneath the ground. By the time summer arrived, El Dorado wouldn't be the same place. He'd already seen it happen in Oklahoma and northern Texas.

Ella put up a fuss and Bridget blushed. How was she supposed to feed her four-month-old daughter in the close quarters of a car with Wyatt not two feet away?

"I expect you'd best stop or she's going to really get loud," Bridget said.

"Why don't I rearrange things so you can sit in the backseat, where you can have more privacy?" Wyatt suggested.

"That would be very nice," Bridget said stiffly.

Wyatt pulled over to the side of the road and hoped he wouldn't get stuck in the soft earth there. Given the condition of the roads, they probably should have taken the train. If Bridget decided she wanted an adventure beyond El Dorado after all, he intended to suggest they house the automobile in a livery and rent a train car so she would be comfortable with Ella.

She stepped gingerly from the front of the vehicle to the back and crawled inside with her daughter. When Wyatt was safely back in the driver's seat and they were on their way again, she unbuttoned her blouse and put Ella to her breast, covering both the baby and herself with a blanket.

"So how long did you live in El Dorado?" Wyatt asked, but he kept his eyes straight ahead on the road. Just knowing what she was doing in the backseat brought a faint blush to his neck. Not that it was repulsive, but a woman nursing her child was such a personal thing, and he felt sorry for her trying to do so in the confines of an automobile with a virtual stranger.

"A little more than a year. I haven't been back since . . . well, since Momma died. I'm hoping that I do not cross paths with any of the Contiello family."

"Where did you live?"

"Not far from town in a huge house almost as big as the Black Swan. Ralph never did anything in a small way. Oh, no, not him. He had the biggest and best of everything," she said.

Wyatt was amazed that she'd opened up even that much to him. "Do you miss that lifestyle?"

"I do not," she said emphatically.

"Why? Big house, lots of maids, money to burn," he said.

"Big house. I cleaned it from top to bottom, with hell to pay if I missed a mote of dust in a corner or a wrinkle in his shirt. Lots of maids? In your dreams. Not even one. That was the wife's job. Clean and iron and make sure Ralph was happy. His mother told me so every sin-gle day when she crossed from her lawn to ours and walked in without knocking on the door. Money to burn? I never had a dime to call my own."

No wonder she was so against men.

"How'd you get home for your mother's funeral?"

"Catherine had come a few weeks before for the trip to the bank. Before she left, she handed me some money and told me to put it away as just-in-case cash. I did, and I used it to come home and get away from Ralph. I wasn't going back. Catherine and I had already discussed my divorce."

Wyatt almost choked. "You are divorced? I thought Ralph just disappeared and you considered yourself a widow."

"I am divorced all legal and proper. Wherever Ralph is, I'm free of him and dang proud of it. I also asked for the O'Shea name back, so it's legal. Ella is not a Contiello. She is an O'Shea," Bridget said.

Holy smoke, the woman had more guts than he'd given her credit for. Going up against an abusive husband and his family and ultimately demanding something he'd never heard of before—her maiden name. Women being granted divorces was practically unheard of, but taking back her name? Now, that took courage.

"Do the Contiellos know about Ella?"

"No, and they aren't going to know either," she said.

What have I gotten myself into? he pondered. He'd met the older Contiellos once at a dinner party when he was soliciting investors into the oil market. They had only met in passing, and he'd like it if he wasn't put into a situation with them again. He'd found out quickly that they had their greedy little fists in other ventures that weren't as clean as crude. He doubted they'd remember him, since they weren't interested in oil.

"So how about you? What do you do in Alvord, Texas?"

"In Alvord. . . ." He pondered a moment, trying to phrase an answer that wouldn't give him away totally. "I've always worked in the family business."

"Which is?"

"Well, it started out that my grandfather owned a general store, and we just grew up in the family business," he said.

"Brothers or sisters?" she asked.

"No sisters. Four brothers."

"I see why you went to the war. A general store wouldn't supply five boys with jobs," she said seriously.

He exhaled in relief. She could continue believing she'd picked up a hobo soldier at the station, and he wouldn't tell her any different. Bridget's experience— divorcing a rich man—suggested that she wouldn't be interested in money, but he'd seen wealth change people too many times. Money steps into a room, and the women all suddenly have dollar signs in their sweet smiles. He wasn't willing to take that chance.

"Why'd you marry Ralph? Did you know he was rich but mean?" he asked.

"Neither. I knew he was comfortable and we wouldn't be poor. I had no idea he was rich or mean. He didn't get ugly until we were married. All goes to show, you can't know a man until you marry him," she said. "And you can't trust them either way."

"Hey, now, don't be making generalizations about men. Not all of them are like that," Wyatt countered.

"I wouldn't take a chance again to prove it one way or the other for all the tea in China or dirt in Arkansas," she said.

That stung. He might not be telling the whole truth and nothing but the truth about his life, but he could be trusted. Not that he gave a tinker's damn what Bridget O'Shea thought of him anyway. The only woman in the world he wanted to impress already had everything money could buy and his best friend wrapped around her little finger.

Bridget had learned the hard way to figure out what Ralph wanted and to have it ready before he could even ask for it, so she recognized the tension that filled the car.

She remembered her advice to Allie Mae, which was to make Orville angry and see how he would react. Bridget found herself in a precarious situation. In her youth she was encouraged to voice her opinion. In her marriage she learned in the first week to keep her mouth shut or pay the consequences. Wyatt was the first man she'd been alone with since Ralph. If she made him mad about something, would he drop her and the car at the hotel and hightail it back to his grandpa's general store? Well, by danged, if he did, she would just put Ella into the backseat and learn to drive home to Huttig. Surely in thirty miles she could get the hang of it.

"Want a cup of coffee or something to drink while we're in Strong?" he asked when they drove into town. There was only one other automobile on the road, but the hitching posts were filled with horses, and several buggies were in sight.

"That would be nice," she said. Evidently she hadn't made him as angry as she thought. If she'd been that abrupt with Ralph, he would have already promised her retaliation when they got home. *Training* was what he called it. A man had to *train* his wife to be submissive and to obey him. He had to *train* her to know what he wanted and how to take care of him even before he asked. If a man had to voice his wishes, then his wife hadn't been *trained* right.

Why are you comparing this man to Ralph? that niggling little voice in the center of her brain asked. *You didn't compare Ira to Ralph or even Quincy, and he was out to send you to jail for murder. So why Wyatt?*

Because I was terrified of Quincy and his authority. Ira was an old friend. And Wyatt is just a man. I don't want him to think I'd ever be interested in another relationship. Not that he's interested in anything other than a job. Oh my, I've got my poor brain so tangled up, I don't know what I'm thinking.

When he parked the car in front of a drugstore, she noticed a Coca-Cola advertisement in the window. Even though it was cold out, and coffee sounded good as a midmorning pick-me-up, suddenly a chilled bottle of Coca-Cola sounded even better. Maybe even with a stick of hard candy, preferably peppermint.

"I'd like one of those and a stick of candy. Let me give you some money," she said.

It went against every grain in Wyatt's body to reach his hand over the backseat and take money from a woman, but in his new role he was a poor hobo with no means. It was either that or give up his true identity.

"I'm going to give you ten dollars. That way you'll have the money to pay for our rooms and food for the next couple of days. Keep track, and if there's any money left, you can give me the change when we get home," she said.

"Yes, ma'am," he said.

"And thanks, Wyatt. It's thoughtful of you to think of what I would want," she said.

"Yes, ma'am," he said again.

It was near lunchtime when they reached the hotel. The busboy carried their bags up to two adjoining rooms and informed them that lunch was being served in the hotel restaurant. Dinner started at six and was served until eight. It pained Wyatt to tip the boy only a dime, but he sucked up the embarrassment and played his part well.

"The candy and Coca-Cola helped, but I am really getting hungry. I forget how much I sample all morning when Allie Mae and I are cooking. So could we please go on down to the café and have lunch?" Bridget asked.

"It's your call. I'm your chauffeur and bodyguard, remember?"

"Then let's go," she said.

The hotel barred no expense in its restaurant. Tables were laid with the finest linen cloths. The silverware was ornate and heavy. Candles were lit in the middle of every table, and the dinnerware was of the finest china. Fancy menus inside a leather-bound folder. No wonder Catherine liked coming to El Dorado.

In the year she'd lived there, Bridget had never been inside that hotel restaurant. When she and Ralph socialized, it was with the rest of his family and always at a home, where the men sat in the yard while the women stayed in the kitchen. The children played, and the mothers took care of them. She never asked what the men discussed and learned early on that her opinion was worthless in the house.

She felt like a princess when Wyatt pulled out a chair for her.

At least until she looked across the room and saw her ex mother-in-law glaring right at her.

Chapter Five

Wyatt studied the menu and decided he'd have a steak dinner with mashed potatoes and green beans. When he glanced up, Bridget looked as if she were in a panic. Her eyes had turned true green and were darting around like those of a scared rabbit's, desperate for a hole to escape a big, mean wolf.

An older woman moved across the room toward them. She had jet black hair pulled tightly away from her face and fastened into a no-nonsense bun at the nape of her neck. Her navy dress was styled with a high white collar edged in lace and white buttons down the front. Lace-up shoes and the inch or so of stockings showing between the hem of her dress and shoe tops were both black.

She had set her eyes on their table and was halfway there when Wyatt realized she was Mrs. Contiello. He was so busy hoping she didn't blow his cover that he forgot all about Bridget.

She stopped a foot from the table and pointed at Bridget. "What are you doing here?"

Bridget looked her right in the eye and held her chin steady. "Having dinner. And you?"

"I told my son that you were trash. Already with another man, and that child has to be five months old, which means you were expecting it when you divorced Ralph. I hope you didn't give her the Contiello name," she said.

"This is my daughter, Ella, and, no, I did not name her Contiello," Bridget said.

"And who is the father?"

"I am," Wyatt said quietly. "If you will excuse us, I'd like to have dinner with my family, and you are interrupting, madam."

"I knew it. Ralph was too lenient on you, Bridget. He failed at your training. He should have taken you in hand and shown you who was boss," Mrs. Contiello said.

"Good day, Mrs. Contiello," Bridget said. "I think I would like to have fried chicken and mashed potatoes and for dessert a slice of rhubarb pie."

Wyatt motioned for the waiter. "I will order it for you."

The older woman didn't move an inch. "I'm not through."

"Yes, ma'am, you are. Ralph is your son, and you love him, but I'm no longer a part of your family, so please leave me alone," Bridget said.

"This isn't over and won't be until we find Ralph. I know you killed him, and I know you and those Irish sisters of yours got rid of his body. It'll surface one of these days, and there's no statute of limitations on murder. You will be punished," she said loudly.

"You find that body and prove I killed him, and I'm sure I'll be punished, but right now I'm having dinner, so please leave," Bridget said.

Mrs. Contiello ignored Bridget and glared at Wyatt. "Be careful. Just because you have a child with her doesn't mean she won't kill you in your sleep. And she's a wild one, that one is, so you'll have to teach her submission. My Ralph couldn't train her to stay in her place, but, bless his heart, he did try. If he could have, he'd be alive today."

"Thanks for the warning, but I think we have a different relationship than she had with your son," Wyatt said.

"If you do, that means she wears the pants," Mrs. Contiello huffed, and she marched out of the restaurant.

A bit of color returned to Bridget's face. She gazed down at her red-haired, blue-eyed child and gave thanks that Ella looked more like her maternal grandmother than the paternal one. Then she glanced up and across the table at Wyatt, who busied himself with the menu, trying to decide which dessert to order.

"Thank you," she said simply.

"For what?"

"You know what for. If that woman thought Ella was her grandchild, she'd try to take her from me."

"I would think, then, that I prevented a killing. I can't imagine you letting anyone take Ella from you without a fight to the death." Wyatt grinned.

"You're very right," she said.

"Did Ralph have black hair and brown eyes?" Wyatt asked.

Bridget nodded.

"You're a lucky woman, Miz O'Shea. I'm surprised that Ella has red hair and blue eyes with a natural father like that."

"God smiled on me the day she was born. I'd decided to have a daughter. I don't know anything about boy children, and I prayed that she would look like my mother, who was also named Ella."

"Well, honey, you got your miracle."

"I did, and I promised not to ask for another one, but I was about to break that promise when I saw Mrs. Contiello coming to our table," Bridget said.

"Enough about a bad subject. Let's enjoy our dinner, and then we'll go to the bank and see if they have time for your business today or if you need to make an appointment for tomorrow. Afterward you can shop to your heart's content. Just remember we only have a little bit of room to take things back," he said.

"Catherine came on the train and had her purchases shipped to Huttig. I expect I can do the same," she said.

"You are the boss," he said.

"I suppose I am," she said absently.

Ella squirmed and looked around the room inquisitively, seeing everything through the eyes of a four-month-old child who was just realizing that there was a whole world out there with pretty colors and sounds. Bridget propped her up on one knee and ate with one hand when her food arrived.

"Not bad but not as good as what you make," Wyatt said.

"Momma liked to cook. She kept us in the kitchen with her so we learned, but it's nice to eat something prepared by another person," she said.

"So what are you going to do if the hotel business ever drops off?" he asked.

"Catherine says I don't have to worry about that. She says Momma and Papa put enough profits into the bank to take care of us. We don't have expensive tastes, so we can manage for a long time even if the mill closes down completely, which I don't think it will do," Bridget said.

"And why's that?"

"It was there before the war, and the town was built before the war. During the war years there was more work, so more men worked there. I expect it will go back to the level it was before the war and stay there. People will always need wood to build houses and businesses. And they'll need to come to Huttig occasionally to make deals, which will require them to stay in a hotel."

Wyatt was mildly surprised to hear her express such well thought-out opinions. Maybe she wasn't as unstable as people said. He thought about water. Yes, if it was spilled carelessly from a glass, it went everywhere and made quite a mess. However, water didn't have to be contained in a glass. The ocean was water, and it had moods and attitudes like a woman's. Surly and angry one day, with breakers slapping against the shore; still and calm the next, with gentle waves kissing the beaches and teasing the kids' toes as they darted in and out.

"Whatever are you thinking about?" she asked.

"Actually, I was thinking about the ocean. Why?" he asked.

"Your mind was somewhere a million miles away from Arkansas. Have you ever seen the ocean?"

He nodded.

She sighed.

"I've always wanted to see it. Catherine went with Quincy to the Gulf of Mexico before they were married. All the way to Florida, and she loved it. I just can't imagine standing on the shore and looking at water that stretches out to the end of the world."

"The sunsets over it are beautiful beyond words," he said.

Bridget couldn't begin to visualize such beauty.

"Want to go?" he asked.

"Of course, but I have a hotel to run and a baby to take care of," she said.

"And it's winter, and there are no guests," he said. A little train trip would take up most of two weeks, and he rather liked the bodyguard business. It would be fun to see Bridget's eyes when she saw the water for which she was named. There was no doubt in his mind that the elder Ella O'Shea had not named her daughters for a flower pot full of earth, a lungful of air, or a glass of water. She had named them for much, much more.

The mere idea of such an impromptu adventure gave Bridget hives. She could feel the itch on her belly and under her winter chemise. On one hand she couldn't fathom such a thing, but Catherine had done exactly that. One day she'd come home from El Dorado, and the next she was on a train with Quincy. But she and Quincy were in love and just had to get away from everything and everyone, especially the place where Ralph had disappeared, and that made it all right. Alice had done something similar the day she boarded the train and went to Grace, Mississippi, to visit Ira. But again, she and Ira were in love. Bridget didn't love or even like Wyatt Ferguson. She was grateful to him for the lie he'd just told about being Ella's father, but she certainly had no amorous feelings for him. And a lady, even a divorced one—perhaps especially a divorced one—did not go out on a lark with an unmarried man. It simply was not done.

But the allure was great as she pictured such a trip and the wind from off the ocean sweeping across her face. Why couldn't Ralph have taken her to see the water instead of being so danged mean?

They made a stop in their rooms after dinner so Bridget could nurse Ella and change her wet diaper. She washed it out in the bathroom located at the end of the hallway and draped it over the chairs and washstand bar in her bedroom. She carefully redressed Ella, putting two diapers on her instead of one and wrapping her in double blankets to protect her against the cold. By the time she knocked on Wyatt's door to let him know she was ready to go to the bank, Ella had already wiggled free of the blankets.

They walked two blocks to the bank in a cold wind coming from a gray sky. Rain was so imminent, Bridget could smell it. She loved rainy days but only when she could stay inside the hotel, not when it was cold and she had to be outside with Ella. Once inside, Wyatt reached for the baby, and Bridget looked at him as if he'd suddenly sprouted horns and a long forked tail.

"I'm not going to hurt her. You'll have papers to sign and business matters to attend to. We'll sit over there in one of those wing chairs where you can see us. That way if anyone in this place knows your former in-laws, they can carry the message back that I'm comfortable with a baby, so she must indeed be mine," Wyatt whispered.

She handed Ella to him slowly. Other than Allie Mae and her sisters, few people ever held the child. Not that they didn't want to, but Bridget always made an excuse. Ella was hers and hers alone, and she didn't have to share if she didn't want to.

The business took the better part of an hour, and Bridget was amazed at the amount of the check she was able to send to Alice. Catherine didn't need the money, so her share was deposited into a savings account right there.

The rest of the profits were Bridget's to do with whatever she wanted, and she had no idea what she wanted other than to see the ocean and breathe in the salt air.

When she finished, she carefully folded the money and put it inside a zippered pocket in her purse. For just a little while she wanted to hold it to realize that it was indeed her money. Tomorrow morning she'd come back to the bank and deposit all but a few dollars into her savings account. Someday Ella would have a nest egg so she could go to college. Maybe by the time Ella grew up, women would have the right to be whatever they wanted. Maybe by then she could even take off on a lark to see the ocean with a man she'd known not even a week, and the whole world wouldn't stop turning on its axis.

She shook hands with the banker and crossed the lobby to where Wyatt held Ella comfortably on his lap, talking to her as if he were indeed her father. Bridget shuddered at the thought of what life would have been like for Ella if Ralph was still around. At that very moment Bridget was especially glad that he was gone, because the first time he hit Ella would have been the day she would have killed him for sure.

Bridget's mother used to say that everything happened for a reason and that God's timing was perfect, even if we didn't think so at the time. She also said that five or ten years down the road after an incident you could look back and see why it had happened. After only a year down the road Bridget already could look back and understand. She'd been pregnant that day she left El Dorado with no intention of ever returning. Had she stayed or been coerced into going back out of pure fear, Ella's life would have been as horrible as hers had been. Looking back, everything *had* happened for a reason, and already she could understand why.

But why is Wyatt Ferguson in my life right now? she pondered as she reached out and held Ella close.

"You'll have an answer when the timing is right, not on your own schedule, Bridget Joy O'Shea." It was her mother's whisper, as close as if she were truly standing right beside Bridget, but she didn't jump and look because it wasn't an unusual phenomenon. Often her mother answered a mental question, and most of the time it was with an answer Bridget didn't really want to hear.

"All done?" Wyatt asked.

"Yes, I am." Her tone was irritable.

"Not a good quarter for the hotel?"

"That isn't a bit of your business, but even though we aren't getting a steady rush of guests for the hotel, the restaurant has had a wonderful quarter," she said.

"Then what are you angry about?"

"I'm not," she protested.

"Have it your way. What now?"

"Let's go to the stores. I lived here for a year and hardly ever got to go anywhere and never alone," she said.

So that's the reason she was so tetchy. The whole

place brought back memories, both physically painful and mentally degrading. Wyatt figured that if he'd been in her shoes for that year, he might have a burr in his saddle too, so he merely nodded and held out his arm.

Reluctantly she slipped her free arm through his. To all the other bank clients they would appear to be a young couple with a new baby. To the man on the far side of the lobby who'd been following them, they'd exchanged a few barbs and weren't really happy in their marriage. At least that's what he will tell Mrs. Contiello, who'd paid him to bring her a report at the end of the day. She wanted to know if her former daughter-in-law had actually married the tall, blond, prosperous-looking man.

They went to the general store, where Wyatt held Ella again. Bridget made decisions about fabric for Ella's new dresses, tablecloths for the restaurant, and new salt and pepper shakers, since several had been broken and needed replacing, and at the very end she splurged on a new store-bought dress in sprigged green ivy with a broad white collar edged in Battenberg lace.

They had ice cream in the middle of the afternoon at a drugstore on Main Street. Wyatt swiped a bit onto the end of his forefinger and put it into Ella's mouth. She smacked and licked her lips.

"That might not be good for her," Bridget said.

"When do they start eating real food?" he asked.

"You haven't ever been around babies?" she asked.

"Not as an adult. I was two when my brother was

born and four when the next one came along. There's one two years older than me and Reuben is four years older. That'd make him thirty on his next birthday. The youngest is Clayton, and he's twenty-one. None of us is married or has children."

"Five kids in—what?—eight years? Bless your momma's heart. And all boys. What sin did she commit?" Bridget said.

"My mother is a saint. She committed no sins, and she did a fine job of raising five boys."

Bridget raised an eyebrow and cocked her head slightly to one side. "Papa didn't have anything to do with raising five boys?"

"My father had a lot to do with raising us. He supported us well and was home in time for supper every night," Wyatt said defensively.

"And was he a strict disciplinarian who made you sit up straight and not use the wrong fork?" Bridge asked.

Wyatt shook his head. "My father is the kindest man you'll ever meet. He believed that you didn't spoil a kid with too much love but with too little discipline. And by 'discipline' I don't mean a belt or a razor strop."

Bridget was suddenly curious. "What did it mean?"

Wyatt grinned.

One layer of ice melted around her heart.

"Well, I remember once I lied to him. I'd been told to weed Momma's flower beds. I was about six, and that was my job, and Dad said a person was known by how well he did his job. He also said that if I wanted the privileges my next older brother got, then I had to show some responsibility. I'd meant to pull the weeds, but then I got to playing, and you know the rest of the story."

"I don't. Tell me." She ate the ice cream slowly, enjoying every bite. But even more than the cold on her scratchy throat, she loved sitting in the drugstore without fear.

"Well, Dad punished me."

"I thought you said he didn't beat you," Bridget said.

"He didn't. He arose early in the morning and had breakfast with Mother. It was summertime, and I wasn't in school yet. So my punishment was that every morning for a week I had to get up with him. I had to eat breakfast before dawn and be at the flower beds when the sun came up. And he checked them every night to see if I'd missed a sprig of grass. I hated that, because grass could grow between the time I weeded and evening. After the first day I'd carefully check every bed just before Dad came home."

"At the end of a week what happened?"

"He declared I was the best gardener in the family and let me go back to sleeping later," Wyatt said.

"Sounds like something my father would have done," she said.

"So you didn't know anything about abusive relationships when you married Ralph?"

"Lord, no. Papa adored Momma. He referred to her as his Irish angel. He had a temper, so don't think he was perfect. He'd get to talking politics and slam a fist on the table. Broke more than one sugar bowl that way. He was passionate in his beliefs and had an opinion on everything. A true Irishman, but he'd never raise his hand to Momma or one of us girls," Bridget said.

"So you literally got blindsided," Wyatt said.

Bridget blinked a few times as she tried to figure out what he meant. "Whatever that means."

"It means that you had a blind spot when it came to Ralph. It never occurred to you that he could be anything other than someone like your father, who was a good husband, adored your mother, and, although he was loud in his opinions, wasn't mean. So you expected Ralph to be the same."

"What made you so smart?" she asked.

"Weeding flowers at daybreak gives a boy a lot of time to think," he teased.

"I had no idea that a marriage could be so miserable. Being with Ralph was like living with two men. One was nice; the other, horrible. The bad one completely overshadowed the good one, and I grew to hate both. I was glad when he disappeared and even gladder when my divorce was granted. If he should ever come back, I'm rid of him," Bridget said.

"Enough philosophizing and thinking about unpleasant things—even if they were brought to the surface because you lived in El Dorado. Let's take Ella back to the hotel and let her have a nap in a real bed where she can stretch out before dinner. You want to eat in the dining room there at the hotel again or go somewhere else?"

"Right there is fine. Actually, I seem to have a bit of a sore throat, so I'll be glad for a nap too. Maybe it will help," she said.

Fifteen minutes later she'd shed her shoes and stockings and was lying on the bed with Ella curled up in the crook of her arm. She nursed until she fell asleep, and Bridget gently readjusted her to one side of the bed, propping pillows around her. Lately Ella had taken to turning herself from one side to the other, and it was a constant worry that she would fall off the bed. Then Bridget fluffed up the remaining pillow and shut her eyes.

Sleep didn't come instantly. Instead she replayed the day and realized that she'd enjoyed Wyatt's company. Other than with her sisters, she couldn't remember the last time she'd been so comfortable with another person. He'd been open and honest, and she'd opened up to him, surprising herself now that she looked at it in retrospect. A friend who was male? Who only wanted a job and nothing more from her?

She fell asleep wondering what she'd see in five years when she looked back.

Wyatt paced the floor of his hotel room, stopping every few minutes to put his ear to the connecting door to make sure Bridget and Ella were all right. Finally he eased the door open and peeked inside. Ella was lying on her stomach with her thumb in her mouth. Without touching the baby, Bridget was curled around her protectively. The window was shut and, he hoped, locked tight. The bolt was thrown across the door, so no one could sneak in that way.

He drew a straight-backed chair over so he could see through the barely cracked door and strained his hearing every time he heard footsteps in the hallway. A few minutes after Mrs. Contiello had left the restaurant, a man had slipped inside and been overly interested in Wyatt and Bridget. He'd tried to cover his slyness by looking at a menu, but too many times his eyes had shifted back to them.

Not that Wyatt was surprised to see a man giving Bridget second glances. She was a lovely lady with that thick, light red hair and luminescent eyes that reflected the color of the ocean. But there were other ladies in the restaurant—a table with four who appeared unattached and very attractive—and the man had never given them a second glance.

Then he had been at the bank and later in the drugstore as they ate ice cream. When they reached the hotel, he was already in the lobby. No doubt about it, Mrs. Contiello had paid someone to report back to her. He just hoped that's all she'd paid him to do.

Chapter Six

At dinner Bridget ordered potato soup and banana pudding for dessert. "My throat is still acting up," she explained. It wasn't fair to get to go into the big town of El Dorado four times a year only to have a sore throat ruin her time there. But such was life, and the next morning she and Wyatt would be on their way back to Huttig. If she didn't feel better, she intended to leave the sign on the door for a couple more days. Allie Mae didn't need to catch a cold, and if Bridget didn't get the illness under control, she wouldn't feel like cooking anyway.

"You need to see a doctor?" Wyatt asked.

"Not over a silly sore throat. I'll go home and have a hot toddy. Likely as not it'll be fine come Monday morning," she said testily.

"Well, don't bite me. I just asked," Wyatt said.

"Don't get all tetchy," she snapped. Exactly why she was being so irritable was a mystery. A sore throat didn't warrant an attitude toward Wyatt. He'd been nothing but nice to her all day. Maybe that was the problem. When Ralph had been nice, there was a storm brewing. Folks said that black clouds had a silver lining. Bridget had learned that big, beautiful, white, fluffy ones had nasty black linings.

He raised both eyebrows. "Me, tetchy? I'm just your employee. A dollar a day and room and board. I've got no reason to care one way or the other if you have a hot toddy or see the doctor or die."

"I'm glad that's clear. After dinner I'm taking Ella back up to our room and resting the rest of the evening. You are free to do whatever men do at night in El Dorado."

"That suits me just fine."

They ate in uncomfortable silence for the rest of the meal. When Bridget finished the last of her banana pudding, she laid her napkin on the table and scooted her chair back. She had a moment of vertigo when she stood up. The floor appeared to be rushing up to meet her, but she attributed it to the sore throat. No doubt it had gotten into her ears and made her a bit dizzy.

Wyatt was immediately on his feet. "You okay?"

"I'm just fine, sir. Finish your dessert. I'm quite capable of finding my room all by myself," she said.

That's when Wyatt saw the man across the room—the same one who'd been following them all day. He almost

sighed at leaving behind half a slice of coconut cream
pie, but the father of Bridget's baby and possibly her
husband wouldn't let her go up to her room alone. So,
playing the part, he reached for Ella and said he was
ready to retire also.

Bridget hugged the baby closer to her chest. "I can
carry my own child."

"And you can also drop her. You are pale, and you
were dizzy. Your eyes actually fluttered back, and you
grabbed the chair for support. Give her to me, and I'll
make sure you're both safe in your room. I'm your bodyguard, remember?"

She passed Ella to him and let him loop her arm
through his for support. It did feel good to know there
was someone strong enough to support her if another
one of those sinking spells came over her. Maybe she'd
keep Wyatt on as a bodyguard forever. A dollar a day
and room and board wasn't exorbitant when she considered how good it felt to have someone to lean on
when she didn't feel well. That's what all women should
do: hire a man to do the necessary chores. Definitely not
marry him, though. Pay him to kill a rat or put a floor in
the basement or provide a big arm to lean on while she
laboriously climbed the stairs.

"Why are you being nice to me?" she whispered.
Heaven forbid she make a scene in a public place. He'd
show his true colors then and pitch a fit, even if he was
just an employee and nothing more.

"Because for a minute there I thought you might be

about to faint. I wouldn't want you to tumble backward down the stairs and hurt the baby," he said. He didn't say that the man on the far side of the dining room stood at the same time they did and was following them up the stairs at a discreet distance.

"I'm not weak," she said.

"Never said you were weak. Said you were dizzy. You want to kill this baby by falling down the steps with her, go right ahead. It's your decision. I'll give her back to you and go have a cigar and an after-dinner drink in the parlor with the other men."

"You're like all the rest of them. Nice one minute. Ugly the next. Thank you for bringing Ella upstairs for me. I'll see you at breakfast in the morning. Eight o'clock in the dining room, and then we'll be off to Huttig," she said.

"You're the boss. I'll be there." The words about his being like all the rest of the men, with Ralph Contiello thrown into the mix, irritated him, but he let it slide. The man keeping tabs on them worried him more than her remarks.

"Good night, Wyatt," she said as she disappeared behind her door.

"Good night, Bridget," he whispered as he opened the door into his room and carefully closed it behind him, leaving just a sliver of a crack. The man who'd followed them upstairs waited for a moment in the hallway and then turned around and headed back down the steps.

The next morning Bridget and Ella entered the dining room promptly at eight o'clock. Her eyes searched the room until she found him. He stood and met her halfway like a good husband/father and took Ella out of her arms. When his hands brushed her wrist, he felt heat that had nothing to do with emotions and everything to do with fever. He studied her face as they made their way to the table he'd claimed. A fine sheen covered her forehead and upper lip. Dark circles rimmed her eyes, and her cheeks were two notches too rosy. Bridget definitely was sick.

"How's the throat?" he asked.

"About the same. I think I'll just have oatmeal for breakfast and some hot tea," she said.

Her voice was softer than usual, giving testimony to the fact that it hurt to talk.

They ate, and he carried Ella up to their rooms so they could finish packing and check out of the hotel. By the time that was done, it had begun to rain—not hard, but the temperature had dropped, and five miles out of El Dorado it started freezing on the windshield. Another three miles and the roads were frozen solid, the ruts and potholes not giving at all when the wheels of the car landed in them. Bridget already felt as if she'd endured one of Ralph's beatings. Every bone in her body ached, and each time Wyatt hit a bump, she let out a small moan.

"Sorry. I'm going as slowly as I can. It's just that the road is so hard, it's a bumpy ride," he said.

"I didn't complain," she shot over the seat.

She was freezing even with her coat buttoned all the

way, a woolen scarf around her neck, and a blanket over her legs. Ella was wrapped up in an extra blanket but kept breaking free with her arms. Thank goodness Bridget had had the foresight to put a tightly knitted sweater on Ella to keep her little arms warm.

Wyatt focused through the freezing rain and on the road so hard that by the time they reached Strong, he had a raging headache. Had there been a hotel in the small town, he'd have been tempted to suggest they stop for the rest of the day and night. But there wasn't. Besides, Bridget was beginning to tremble, which meant her fever was even higher. To the devil with what she wanted. As soon as he got her and Ella safely inside the Black Swan and built a fire in the furnace, he was going for a doctor. A hot toddy might cure a sore throat; it wouldn't touch the flu.

The rain let up slightly for a few miles when they turned off the road in Strong and headed toward Huttig, but the last three miles were nothing but sleet beating against the roof and windshield of the car. Several times Wyatt had to put on the brake and get out of the car to free the wipers, which could not keep up with the weather.

When he finally pulled into the yard at the Black Swan, his back and neck were tense from the drive, his head threatening to split, and all he wanted was a hot bath, a cup of black coffee, and a warm bed. None of which he could have until he had Bridget and Ella warm and a doctor in the house.

"Thank God," she mumbled as she tried to open the rear door.

"You'll have to wait for me to force it. I'm sure it's frozen shut," he said.

"I'd crawl over the back of the seat to get out your door just to be inside and out of this mess," she said.

"You may have to if I can't open this door," he said. But on the third try the ice broke away and the door flew open with such force that he practically landed on his backside.

She slid out and handed him Ella. "Please bring her inside, Wyatt. I'm afraid I'll slip and fall."

"Hold on to my arm. We'll go slowly," he said. The grass crunched under his feet, each blade a sliver of brown inside a sheath of ice. The pine needles bent with the weight of the ice, and every few minutes a crack filled the air that said another branch had broken somewhere.

"Snow was nothing compared to this," she said.

"It'll pass," he tried to reassure her.

"Are you God?" she asked.

"Last time I checked, I was merely a man," he answered tersely.

"Then you don't know that it will pass. It may last forever, and we'll all die frozen in our beds rather than blown up by the Communists. Don't try to make me feel better. I'm not a baby," she said.

"Well, pardon me for breathing," he said.

She just blew out a stream of warm air that seemed to

freeze in front of her face. They made it to the porch and up the slick steps without a mishap, which surprised Wyatt, but he wasn't taking anything for granted. He did not hurry toward the door but chose his footing carefully.

Once inside the cold hotel he handed Ella off to Bridget and went straight to the basement. Building the fire wasn't the job it might have been if they'd stayed gone another day. The embers were still warm, so he stirred them and threw in several sticks of wood. When the fire was well under way, he shut the furnace door and went back up to check on Bridget. She was huddled on a settee with Ella in her lap. Her head was thrown back and her eyes shut. When she heard him stomping across the floor, she opened them.

Wyatt gasped. Her eyes were glazed with fever, and her face was scarlet. She'd removed the scarf and un-buttoned her coat, but her hands trembled as she held Ella. The baby cooed and wiggled, but Bridget kept her hugged tightly, as if she feared she'd drop her if she re-laxed her hold.

"Where's the nearest doctor?" he asked.

"Just make me a toddy," she said. "Whiskey is in the kitchen. Honey is on the table."

"This time, boss lady, I'm calling the shots. Where is the nearest doctor?"

"I'm not paying a doctor to tell me I have a cold. You are paid to do what I say. Make me a toddy."

He ignored her slurred remark and went straight for

the phone. Surely the operator could tell him where to find a doctor. If not, he'd drive down to the Commercial hotel and ask someone there, or to the general store if he had to. Surely Minnie would know.

Bridget tried to yell at him when he picked up the phone and asked the operator to ring up the doctor in Huttig. It came out a hoarse, weak muttering that sounded more like a wounded tomcat than a woman screaming at a man.

"You are fired," she got out.

"That's fine by me, but I won't leave you dying," he said.

That brought her up short. Dying? Good Lord, what would happen to Ella if she died? Alice or Catherine could raise her, and either one would love her, but she should at least have a real mother if she couldn't have a father.

"Yes, sir, this is Wyatt Ferguson. I work at the Black Swan for Bridget O'Shea. I believe she may have the flu," he said into the phone's mouthpiece. He listened for a moment and then said, "Thank you, sir."

"What did he say?" she whispered. The flu: it had passed. No one had had the dread disease in almost a year. Her mother was the last in Huttig to succumb to it. Surely the germs didn't linger that long. They couldn't live for a year and then suddenly infect someone, could they?

"He's on his way. I caught him at the Commercial.

Some man had fallen on the ice and broken his ankle. The doctor was there treating that, so he says he'll be here in twenty minutes."

"Can you watch Ella until he gets here? I'm going to bed," Bridget said.

"I can do that. I'll pack my trunk and catch a ride to the train station with doc after he examines you. I can pack and watch the baby at the same time," he said.

"That's fine with me," she said as she made her way to the back of the lobby and opened the door into her private quarters. Each laborious step brought her closer to her room but took more energy than mere walking should. But the doctor was on the way, and he'd give her some elixir or a dose of something out of his magic black bag, and in a few hours she'd be good as new.

When she reached the bed, she fell on it without removing her coat or her shoes. She curled up in a ball, trying to draw warmth from any part of her feverish body that might give it up. Her teeth began to chatter, so she crammed the corner of a pillow into her mouth. Her stomach rolled and threatened to heave the oatmeal back up. She'd have to get better to even die, because surely she'd bypassed death on her way downward.

By the time the doctor arrived, the hallucinations had begun. Her mother was sitting in the rocking chair knitting a pink sweater, and Bridget kept telling her to hurry because she needed it to keep warm. Her father sat on the edge of her bed and argued that she had to get well because heaven wasn't ready for her.

"Fever is high. She's out of her mind with it, Wyatt. I think it might be the flu. God Almighty, but I'd hoped we'd cleared that hurdle. Okay, here's what I'm going to do. I'll leave this medicine. You give it to her every four hours around the clock. Two teaspoons. It tastes horrible, but make her take it. I'll tell Minnie to send Tommy out here with a couple of cases of that canned milk. Mix one part boiled and cooled water to one part milk for the baby. Bridget won't be feeding her anymore. Guess I'll need to tell Minnie to send a few bottles and nipples too. This hotel is quarantined. No one comes in, and you three don't go out. I'll check on her in a few days, if she lives that long," the doctor said.

"She fired me. I was planning on going to the train station with you," Wyatt said absently.

"Not now you aren't. Not for three weeks at the very least. If it's the flu, you could spread it. Don't let Ella near her for at least a week. You'll have to come into the room and take care of her, but then, you've been with her the whole last week, so you've already been exposed. The baby has too, but there's no need taking unnecessary chances," the doctor told him.

Wyatt felt as if someone had just kicked him in the gut. He had a sick woman and a baby to take care of, and he knew absolutely nothing about either. He should have gone on to Alvord, faced the fact that Ilene was engaged to his best friend, and gotten on with his life instead of running from it.

"I'll leave you a list of things to do to help. Change

her bed every day. Wash the bedding in boiling water. The laundry won't be picking it up because of the infection. The medicine will fight the fever, but it has to run its course. Get as much fluid into her as possible. I'll tell Minnie to leave a chicken on the porch every morning. Boil it and make her drink the broth. The rest is on this list."

The doctor laid it on the clerk's desk. "I've helped her get into a nightgown and put her under the covers. Good luck, Mr. Ferguson. You're about to earn your wages. I sincerely hope you are as strong and healthy as you look and don't catch it."

"Yes, sir, and thank you for coming," Wyatt said.

"You might want to call Catherine or Alice. They both survived it when they took care of their parents."

"I've been exposed now too. I'll just do the best I can," he said.

The doctor nodded and let himself out the front door.

Wyatt tiptoed into the forbidden territory of Bridget's quarters. The living room offered a comfortable sofa and chairs to match, lamps to read by, and a woman's touch everywhere he looked. There was one bedroom on each side. He heard a faint rustling of sheets and peeked into the room where Bridget was covered to her chin. It had to be where the sisters had shared a bedroom. Three full-sized beds, three dressers, three rockers, three desks. A rocking cradle was close to Bridget's bed. Wyatt carefully laid Ella on the sofa and dragged the cradle out into the living room, across the floor, and into the other bedroom. If he was going to be nursemaid for the next three weeks, he'd adjust the living quarters to meet his needs. He and Ella would sleep in the empty bedroom, where he could better hear Bridget through the night. There was a bathroom off the living room, so that would be handy. The first thing on Doc's list that he'd barely scanned was that he should wash his hands every time he came out of her room.

"She's going to be a handful when she finds out she can't see or touch you for at least a week," he told Ella.

The baby cooed and smiled.

"I'm glad to see you with a positive attitude, little lady. When you get hungry and have to take your milk from a bottle, you might not be nearly so happy," he said.

She gave him another big toothless grin.

"Momma, what am I going to do with Ella? I'm so sick," Bridget said in a thin voice.

He stopped in his tracks. Bridget couldn't die. What would happen to that precious baby girl? Her Aunt Catherine or Aunt Alice would take her in, but the child deserved a mother, especially since she sure didn't have a father in her life.

She's delirious. My grandpa got like that before he died. Saw my grandmother who'd been dead for years. Dear God!

"Okay, enough bad thoughts," he said aloud. "That can't help us. We're going up to my room as soon as I get this cradle in here, and I'm bringing my things downstairs. I'll shut off my old room so we don't have to heat it. I'm going to be crazy by the end of the week with only a four-month-old baby to talk to," he said.

He set the cradle beside the double bed in the room that had belonged to the elder Ella and Patrick O'Shea. Their life was before him in little things. A picture of each daughter framed in pewter on the dresser. A book of Irish poetry on a table beside the bed. A pair of reading glasses on the one on the other side.

After a quick glance around the room he carried Ella with him upstairs, only to quickly realize he couldn't carry his trunk and her back down at the same time. He jerked the quilt from the bed and spread it out on the floor, put Ella in the middle of it, and told her to be still in the most authoritative voice he could muster up. He carried the trunk down to the bedroom and raced back up to find that she'd rolled over three times and was on her stomach on the cold floor, licking the hard wood.

"Hey, lady, we'll have none of that. I'll make *you* boil the sheets if I catch you doing that again." Wyatt laughed.

By the time he had changed Ella twice and then realized he would be responsible for diaper cleanup as well as laundering sheets every day, he'd gone looking for washtubs and a washboard. When he found an electric wringer-type washer hidden in a corner of the kitchen, he literally shouted and scared Ella. She puckered her lower lip and whimpered.

"Sorry, darlin'. I'm just glad I don't have to wash everything by hand. I'll run some clotheslines in the lobby to hang the laundry every day. I'm thinking your mommy is going to owe me more than a dollar a day when this is all said and done."

As he and Ella scoped out places to hang ropes for clotheslines, he heard someone knock on the door. By the time he opened it, a hand waved from a truck with *Huttig General Store* painted on the side. Two large boxes had been set on the porch. He tugged them in with one hand while holding Ella with the other.

One was a case of canned milk. The other had three chickens and a beef roast each wrapped in butcher's paper, a box of laundry detergent, and half a dozen baby bottles and nipples, along with a container of BC Headache Powders. The last was the best thing he found in the delivery. In the rush of figuring how on earth he was going to cope with a baby when he had little experience, he'd put aside his headache, but it was definitely still there.

He went to the kitchen and opened one of the papers containing the white powder and stirred it into a glass of cool water. He hated the taste of the medicine, so he downed it in several big swallows. He put the chickens and the roast into the refrigerator, then remembered the doctor's directions about boiling a chicken for broth. He found a pot, filled it with water, and dropped a whole chicken into the water.

"I hope she likes chicken broth, because I've got a feeling if she doesn't, I'll be fired a hundred times in the next three weeks," he said.

Ella began to whimper and nuzzle the front of his shirt.

"I suppose I'd better start a kettle of water to boiling to make you some milk. Boil and then cool. The milk is cold, so the water won't have to be cold. You'll have to be patient with me," he said.

Ella was not patient. By the time he had a bottle ready, she was telling the whole world that she wanted her milk and she wanted it right now. When he finally got the first bottle ready and put the nipple into her mouth, she spit it out and fussed some more.

Bridget heard her daughter crying and wondered who had brought a baby to the hotel. She couldn't remember any of her mother's friends looking as if they were going to have a baby. Women got big and round in the stomach just before a baby was born. She drifted back into a gray fog produced by the vile-tasting medicine the doctor had given her, still wondering whose baby was nearby.

Finally Ella decided that even if what came out of the rubber nipple didn't taste as good as what she was used to, it wasn't too bad. She sucked until she drained the bottle and then promptly went to sleep.

Wyatt tiptoed to the bedroom and laid her ever so gently in the cradle, then checked on Bridget, who was fidgeting with the covers in her sleep, wringing them as if she were trying to make the edges of the blankets produce water.

He sank into the sofa and shut his eyes. "Lord, what have I gotten myself into?"

Not a single answer floated down from the ceiling.

Chapter Seven

Wh* *hile Ella slept, he kept a watch on the chicken, found a handwritten recipe book on the counter, and uncovered the washing machine. It was older than the one his mother used in Alvord, but it had a tub, a motor, and a wringer, and he was grateful he wouldn't have to drag out the washboard and wring sheets by hand.

He checked on the sick woman and the sleeping baby and made a hurried trip to the basement, where he retrieved a hammer, a fistful of nails, and a length of rope. He measured, stepped back, and eyed the places he'd marked for clotheslines in the lobby, and changed his mind. If he put them up that way, he'd have to brush laundry to one side every time he made a trip from the kitchen to Bridget's room. Finally he decided to run the lines from the front door down the length of the room and fasten the other end onto the door frame into the living room. The laundry would only block off the stairs with that configuration, and no one would be going up there anyway. He could brush aside the damp linens twice a day when he went down to the basement to tend the fire. Besides, the lines would cross the main heating vent coming up from the furnace into the lobby, and if he needed faster drying on any items, he could hang them above it. Finally he hammered two nails into each door frame and stretched his ropes good and tight.

"That should hold sheets," he said.

Bridget heard hammering. She figured Ira must be fixing the roof, but he shouldn't be doing that in the winter. It was too dangerous to work when his fingers would freeze and he could hit them with the hammer. She called out to Alice to make him come inside and have some hot chocolate. Her mouth suddenly felt parched. She wanted some hot chocolate herself, or maybe hot tea. Maybe Alice could make her hot tea like she did the night Ralph fell down the steps.

She didn't open her eyes but found a corner of the sheet and worried it into knots while her feverish brain skipped back in time almost a year. There was Ralph storming into the hotel without knocking and breathing fire and screaming threats about what he would do to her for disobeying him. He took the steps two at a time, jerking off his belt in rage as he ascended. She was not going back to El Dorado with him; that had already been decided. She met him at the top of the stairs. Alice came out of a guest room down by the bathroom. Catherine was at the bottom of the stairs by the time he reached the top.

It all happened so fast. One minute he was coming up the steps; the next second he had his hand up to hit her; the next she pulled her mother's little two-shot derringer from her pocket and shot at him. She had missed, and the bullet had landed in a door frame; the hole was still there and reminded her daily of how lucky she'd been not to have hit him. He had been on the top step, and the shot had stunned him. When he had recovered his senses and lunged to slap the fire out of Bridget, he lost his balance and fell, tumbling all the way to the bottom of the staircase.

The silence was deafening. One minute the hotel was in an uproar, where Bridget couldn't hear anything; the next, a feather floating from heaven on an angel's wing would have sounded like a cannon boom. Ralph was dead, and the blood from the back of his head soaked into the rug. It was one her mother had just made, so Bridget always regretted losing that rug, but Alice had said it went to a good cause.

Bridget whimpered in her drug-induced sleep and touched her dry mouth. It was the tea that Alice brewed later that night, after they'd buried Ralph, after they'd wiped up the blood and covered the dark spot with another rug; after it all, it was the tea that soothed Bridget.

Her mind jumped ahead a few weeks to the day Quincy arrived. She started twisting at the sheets again as she remembered that afternoon. They were sitting on the porch having cookies and tea when the sheriff brought Quincy. Who'd have thought Catherine would fall in love with him? Quincy was determined to find Ralph. He dug up everything: the garden, the rose-bushes, the flower beds. If it had a fresh dirt pile, he had a shovel digging at it. Silly man. Ralph wasn't buried on the Black Swan property. But Catherine insisted on letting him dig so he would be able to tell everyone that the O'Shea girls had had nothing to do with Ralph's disappearance.

Finally the visions stopped, and she drifted off into an untroubled sleep, only to awaken to someone prop-ping pillows behind her back and sitting her straight up in bed. For a moment she wondered what on earth she was doing asleep in the middle of the day; then she was angry that someone would wake her in the middle of the night. No sunshine streamed through the lace-covered windows into the room, so it couldn't be daytime.

"Bridget, you have to drink this," Wyatt said.

Her voice was raspy, and when she breathed, her lungs sounded like crinkling newspaper. "Who are you?"

"I'm Wyatt Ferguson, your hired hand. The doctor has quarantined us for three weeks. This is chicken broth, and I've made you a cup of tea. You are to drink both so you can get well," he said.

She tried to wiggle back down into the covers. "I fired you. Go away."

"Well, at least you remember that much. Drink or I'll pour the danged stuff down your throat," he said.

She opened her eyes and tried to fry him on the spot with a look. It didn't work, so she opened her mouth and allowed him to spoon in warm broth. It had no taste at all and could have been nothing more than hot water, but it helped quench the parched thirst she felt would kill her.

"If I hold it, can you drink this tea without using a spoon?" he asked.

"I can do anything. I can run this hotel. I told Catherine and Alice I could, and I will. All by myself. You are fired," she said.

"I'd love to be fired. Nothing would suit me better, but I'm stuck in this hotel with you for three weeks, so stop firing me and drink this."

Her hands trembled, and he had to help her keep the cup steady, but she managed to finish it. "More, I want more tea."

"Then you'll have it. The water is already hot. Give me two minutes to steep it, and I'll be right back."

"Bathroom." She blushed, turning her face even more crimson than the fever had.

Wyatt felt a hot flush creeping up his neck. He could wash the sheets and change the baby's diaper, but how did he handle this one?

"Help me," she said.

He pushed back the covers, picked her up like a

bride, and carried her to the bathroom door. "I'm going to set you down now. You'll have to take care of things by yourself. Be careful. If I hear you fall, I will come in there."

"And if you do, I swear I'll kill you," she whispered.

"Darlin', you'll have to get a lot stronger than you are now to kill me."

"Don't call me darlin'."

She stumbled into the bathroom and braced herself on the sink before kicking the door shut in his face. The woman looking back at her in the mirror wasn't Bridget. She was a hollow-eyed, sunken-cheeked witch with limp hair falling out of the bun on top of her head. Just the morning before she'd been well except for a sore throat. Great God in heaven, what would she look like tomorrow morning if only a day could wreck such havoc?

She found a washcloth, wet it, and washed her face. She took down her hair and braided it into two long ropes. And then she remembered why she was in the bathroom. It took the rest of her energy to edge over to the toilet. The only thing that kept her from falling into a heap was Wyatt Ferguson's promise to come into the bathroom with her if he heard a thump.

Wyatt waited, his ear plastered to the door, and only stepped back in time to avoid being hit when she swung it open. In his estimation she was even more pale and fragile.

"I can walk to my bed," she announced.

Two steps later he caught her as she began to sink. "Not this time. Maybe another day."

"Am I going to die?" she asked when he had her tucked back into bed.

"I hope not."

She looked around the room in a panic. "Where's Ella?"

"Ella is fine. She's on a pallet because she's rolling from one side to the other, and I'm afraid she'll roll off the bed or upset the cradle. You cannot see her until you are well. Doctor's orders."

"Bring me my child right now," she ordered.

"I should have known you weren't going to be a nice patient," he said.

"You work for me, not for Doc. Bring me Ella. She'll starve."

"She's eating from a baby bottle very well. Half boiled water that's been cooled, half canned milk. We've managed two feedings already today. No tummyaches or screaming, so I guess she's not starving," he said.

"Call Catherine," she said.

"Why? So she can come here and catch the flu and die? We are quarantined. No one comes in, and no one goes out. Get used to it, Bridget. We're stuck with each other for three weeks. And now it's time for your medicine. I'll brew that cup of tea so you can have it afterward. The stuff smells so bad that I can't imagine putting it in my mouth."

"I'm not taking any more. It makes me dream," she said.

"Dream or die? Your choice. Make up your mind before I get back with the tea."

Who'd have ever thought one little Irish lass could be so danged bullheaded? he thought as he made tea and carried it back to her bedside.

She glared at him.

He just shrugged. "Which did you decide? There's no use wasting a good cup of tea if you are going to die."

"Give me the stuff and go away. You'd better take good care of Ella while I'm sick, or I'll send you away without a dime," she said weakly.

He poured the medicine into a spoon and watched her literally shiver from head to toe when she swallowed it. He held her hands while she drank the second cup of tea and watched as her eyelids grew heavier and heavier until she was asleep and worrying the covers again.

The whole living room smelled like an outdoor toilet when he shut the door to Bridget's room. Ella was on her back cooing at something on the ceiling while she kicked her legs and arms. Wyatt's nose wrinkled, and he moaned. Before that day he'd only changed one diaper in his entire life, and that had been with lots of help. Granted, he'd won the five-dollar bet, and at the time it had seemed worth it, but since they'd gotten back from El Dorado, he'd already changed Ella five times from the skin out. His pay was still only a dollar a day, and right then he would have gladly given a whole week's paycheck if Allie Mae would come along and take care of this smelly mess.

He was quite proud of himself for only gagging once during the episode. But then, he'd taken the easy way out. He removed all Ella's clothing, dropped it in a pile on the pallet, and picked Ella up under her arms, holding her away from him. She thought it was a big game and giggled when he laid her in the bathtub, ran the water until it was warm, and then used a cup to rinse her clean. She giggled every time he poured a cupful over her body, so he took the opportunity to give her a soapy bath.

He'd just wrapped her in a bath sheet when he heard a heavy pounding on the front door. Surely any prospective guest could see the quarantine sign the doctor had tacked to the front porch post. He and Ella hurried across the floor to peek out from behind the lace door curtain. There was Clark at the edge of the yard, pointing to a box on the porch and waving.

Wyatt waved back and eased the door open far enough to drag the wooden box inside. The note stuffed down inside read: *We heard Miss Bridget has the flu. You'll have your hands full taking care of her and the baby, so Minnie or me will set a box on the porch every other day so you don't have to cook. It's important to make Bridget eat. Those who wouldn't eat last year died. There's chicken and dumplings in the jars. Chocolate cake in the pan. If you'll wash the jars and pans and put them back in the box, then leave them on the porch, I'd appreciate it. Lizzy, the lady next door.*

Wyatt could have kissed Clark's mother for thinking of them. He let the food set long enough to take Ella back to the bedroom and dress her—one more time. He made her a fresh pallet and laid her on her stomach, then went back to the lobby to take care of the food. His stomach growled, and he remembered that he hadn't eaten since breakfast.

He poured a jar of dumplings into a pan to heat and ran a finger along the edge of the cake. "God bless good neighbors."

He kept one ear trained toward the living room while he prepared the food and then carried it in to watch the baby while he ate. He peeked in on Bridget twice, and she was sleeping soundly. By the time he swallowed the last bite of cake, Ella had begun to scrub at her eyes and fuss.

"You're hungry again too?" he asked.

She gave him a wide-eyed look that resembled her mother's so much that Wyatt grinned. He picked her up, relieved that she was still dry, and carried her with him to the kitchen.

"You're going to break lots of little boys' hearts."

She cooed.

"Starting with this old man's heart," he sighed.

She fell right to sleep after nursing a full bottle of milk, and Wyatt put her in her cradle, which he'd pushed right up next to the bed he intended to sleep in that night. Dark came early, but he wasn't the least bit sleepy. It was still a couple of hours before Bridget's next dose of medicine, so he paced awhile, looked out at the moon rising over a frozen world, and wished for a book or a current newspaper.

Finally he found himself pacing through the kitchen for the fifth time and took a long, hard look at the washing machine. No one said laundry had to be done in the daytime or on Monday morning. Why not do it now, let it dry all night, take it down in the morning, and get ready for a new day? He pulled the machine out, set water to boiling on the stove, and hoped like the devil he could remember how his mother did laundry.

In two hours he had all of Ella's clothing and diapers washed and hanging in the lobby. He ran a hose out the kitchen window and let the wash water flow across the yard while a new batch of water boiled and got ready for Bridget's sheets. At the right time he checked on Ella— who apparently was down for the night, or at least until the middle-of-the-night feeding—and went into Bridget's room.

Her eyes were wide open and her breathing shallow. For a moment he thought she was at her last, until her eyelids snapped a few times and she gave him one of those drop-dead looks.

"Don't tell me it's time for that vile stuff again." Her voice was still raspy, and the syllables came out individually rather than as smooth words flowing into a whole sentence.

"Not just yet. First you are going to eat and then go to the bathroom and wash up while I change your bedding."

"Bed is clean. I just changed it a couple days ago."

"Your Irish is showing."

She pulled the covers tighter around her neck. "You're crazy. Nothing is showing."

"Your Irish temper is showing big-time. Doc says this bed is to be changed daily. I'm choosing to do the changing at night so you'll have a clean bed to sleep in. Besides, if I change it at night, I can wash the linen, and it can dry overnight," he explained.

"Send it to the laundry," she said.

"No one comes in or out. Remember?"

It took several minutes for that to sink into her foggy brain. Surely Catherine and Alice had sent out the laundry when her father and mother were ill with the flu. No, no, they hadn't. Bridget hadn't been there in those days. She'd been in El Dorado, and Alice said she was glad they could finally put the washing machine back in the corner. Suddenly Bridget remembered that Wyatt would have to wash dirty diapers. She didn't know whether to laugh or blush. He was danged sure going to earn that dollar a day!

"Lizzy over next door sent chicken and dumplings. You are going to eat some," Wyatt said.

Bridget had never liked dumplings. They were nothing but dough balls cooked in chicken broth, and she despised the slimy texture. She'd never even liked her mother's dumplings, which were the fluffiest and best in the world. She wrinkled her nose and turned her head toward the wall.

"Evidently you don't like dumplings," he said.

"Hate them. Just tea please."

"Chicken broth and tea, but only if you try a piece of toasted bread," he said.

She nodded.

The way he figured it, dumplings were dough, and bread was dough, so what was the difference in nutrition? He prepared her supper and took it to her on a tray: a slab of bread he'd buttered and toasted in an iron skillet, a cup of broth, and hot tea with extra sugar.

He set it before her and, using a knife and fork, fed the bread to her as if it was a steak. When she refused to eat any more after two bites, he shook his head.

"No, ma'am. Either the whole piece or dumplings it is," he said.

"You are the devil."

"Honey, I might be, but you will eat. Lizzy said that's what makes the difference in getting better or dying."

"I'm not going to die."

"That's the gospel truth. You'd have to get a sweeter nature before Lucifer would have you—and forget about getting through the Pearly Gates. Heaven isn't ready for a spitfire like you. Eat."

She opened her mouth. It took too much energy to chew. She asked for the broth and sipped it awhile, then allowed him to feed her another bite. That seemed to work better. A couple of bites of toast, then two or three sips of broth while she regained strength to chew again.

Her, a spitfire? Now that was something to think

about while she let the medicine throw her back into oblivion. She'd been called a lot of things but never a spitfire.

"Ella?" she said between sips.

"She's sleeping. She's had a bath. Actually, it was a necessary bath. I can't imagine getting her clean any other way," he said.

Bridget almost smiled, but the agony of not seeing her daughter was more than she could bear. She was almost glad that Ella had caused Wyatt extra work. It was his penance for being able to hold Ella and love her when Bridget could do neither.

"Enough. I'll bring it all up if you make me eat more today," she declared.

"Okay, then to the bathroom while I change your sheets." He picked her up and carried her across the bedroom and living room, depositing her gently just outside the bathroom door.

"I forgot my things. I've got to go back. I feel so sticky."

He picked her up again and took her back to the bedroom, where she opened a drawer and brought out clothing. She held the items close to her chest when he scooped her up again. No way was he going to lay eyes on her cotton drawers and nightgown. Then she felt a slow heat crawling up her neck. Wyatt Ferguson would be washing both underdrawers and nightgowns along with sheets every day until she got well. That was every bit as humiliating as covering bruises on her legs and arms so no one could see that she'd been beaten.

Wyatt checked on Ella again while he waited. Surely if Bridget had the deadly strain of flu, she'd be worse instead of better at the end of the first day. But then, he'd been blessed not to lose a family member when the epidemic hit, so he knew little about it. Maybe tomorrow was the worst day or the one after that. They didn't quarantine a house for three weeks for nothing.

He went back to her bedroom, stripped the linens away, and began the search in dresser drawers for fresh sheets. The first one he opened netted him nothing but emptiness. So did the second. The third was the charm. He made the bed with good tight corners and a top sheet and two quilts, replaced the pillow cases, and had it turned down, ready for her, when he heard the bathroom door open.

She'd made it halfway across the floor when he reached her. "You should have called me."

"I can walk better than I can scream. Let me lean on you. Layin' in bed will just make me weak. I don't have the flu. I'm just sick. If I had the flu, I'd be worse, and I think I'm better after two doses of medicine."

He wrapped an arm around her and helped her back to bed.

"You won't get out of taking this dose by saying you don't have the flu." He picked up the medicine and poured a dose.

She shuddered but opened her mouth, then motioned for the tea.

"I hate the feeling it brings as much as the taste," she said.

"Kind of muddled?"

"Worse. I have no control."

"I'm sure that's horrible. The wicked witch of southern Arkansas with no control."

"Don't tease me."

"Just sleep. Rest. Eat. Get better. Maybe we'll be lucky and you don't have the flu. Doc said he'd be back in a week but that, no matter what, he's leaving us in quarantine for three weeks just to be safe."

She snuggled down into clean sheets. "By then I'll be crazy."

"After one day I already am. You'll have to run to catch up with me on that issue."

Her eyelids went heavy, and she shut them. But this time she didn't dream about Ralph. Instead she and Wyatt were running across warm sand. Ella was a toddler and played on the seashore with a bucket, gathering sand and pouring it out. Bridget was lucid enough to wish she had told Wyatt that she would go with him to see the ocean. If the flu did kill her, at least she would have smelled the salt water before she died.

Chapter Eight

Exactly a week later they faced off from opposite sides of Bridget's bedroom.

Bridget was fully dressed in her overalls and a white blouse, her hair done up properly in a bun on top of her head. A few wisps had escaped and fanned out around her face, giving her an impish look.

Wyatt had his back to the door, daring her to take another step forward. There was no way she was getting outside the room until the doctor arrived and pronounced her well enough to be around Ella. Not after he'd washed dirty diapers all week, boiled a chicken every other day, and all but begged her to swallow the vile medicine.

"I'm well, and I'm getting out of this room before I go crazy. Did I tell you I'm named for water? It doesn't like being cooped up, and I'm going out there into the living room, and I'm holding my baby," she declared.

"You're staying in this room with the door shut until the doctor comes."

She set her jaw and spoke through clenched teeth. "I'll fight you, and I'll win."

"You are five feet three inches if you count that knot on top of your head. You might weigh a hundred and ten pounds soaking wet. I could tie one arm behind me and still barricade this door."

"Hello! Anyone at home?" a masculine voice yelled from the lobby area.

"Doc's here," Wyatt said. "We'll see what he has to say."

"I don't give a hoot what he has to say. I'm well, and I'm . . ."

Wyatt opened the door and motioned for the doctor. "Come on back, Doc. We're in the bedroom."

"Don't suppose she died or we'd have had a funeral at the church by now. Is the baby all right, and how are you?" the doctor asked.

"I'm fine. Ella's fine. Bridget is meaner than a hungry rattlesnake."

The doctor sat down in the rocking chair and opened his worn black bag. "Sit down on the edge of the bed right here in front of me," he told Bridget.

Bridget shot Wyatt a drop-dead look and plopped down.

The doctor listened to her lungs, front and back, as

well as her heart. "Well, you must have the luck of the Irish working for you. I would have sworn you'd be dead by now or at least still too sick to put up a fight. If this was the flu, it wasn't the same kind as last year's. But just to be on the safe side, I'm going to leave the hotel under quarantine for the full three weeks. That means two more weeks before you go out or anyone comes inside. How long has it been since she's had a fever?" He looked at Wyatt.

"Two days. First three days she'd rouse up enough every four hours to be hateful and eat a little bit. I'd give her the medicine, and it would knock her out for another four hours. The past two days she's been fever free, but I made her take the medicine anyway. You got any that'll knock her out for eight hours at a stretch for the next two weeks?"

"I won't take another dose of that vile stuff. I'd rather kiss old Lucifer on the end of his pointy tail than take any more of it," Bridget declared.

A grin ironed out a few of the old doctor's wrinkles. "I'd say you don't need any more medicine, Bridget, and you can do whatever you feel up to doing. Mr. Ferguson, you won't need to wash the bed sheets every day, but you can't send out laundry for another two weeks with the quarantine. And after the quarantine is lifted, I want every square inch of the place scrubbed with soap before you let any guests back into the place. That's just to be on the safe side."

"We did that after Momma died, so we can do it

again. Now, may I please go outside this room and hold my baby?" she asked.

"She still on the bottle?" the doctor asked.

Bridget's chin quivered. "And will be from now on. My milk dried up while I was sick."

"It won't hurt her. Might give her some applesauce or pureed pears along with it." He snapped his bag shut.

"How much do I owe you?" Bridget asked.

"Take two dollars off my restaurant bill. I'll see you in another week just to make sure you're still fine and the other two in this house are the same," he said.

Wyatt swiftly crossed the living room, went into his and Ella's bedroom, and picked her up from the cradle where she was having her morning nap. His mother had often said that sleeping babies should not be disturbed, but in this case Ella could either sleep later or be cranky.

Bridget met him in the middle of the living room with outstretched hands. For a moment he held Ella close to his chest, hating to share her. One more tight hug and he handed her over to Bridget, who had tears streaming down her face.

"What if she wakes up and doesn't remember me?" she whispered.

"A baby never forgets its momma. It's a law of nature." Wyatt just hoped that Ella didn't forget *him* now that she had her mother back.

Ella opened her blue eyes and stared at Bridget, cocking her head to one side and then the other. Finally she gave her mother a big two-toothed grin and snuggled against her breasts.

"When did she get teeth?" Bridget asked.

"They popped through a couple of days ago. The process produced a ton of slobbering, though. I don't know which got wetter—her bibs or her diapers," he said.

"I missed it! I missed her first teeth." The dam let go, and Bridget wept against Ella's shoulder.

"It wasn't any big deal. She gnawed on her fist, and then, day before yesterday, they broke the skin. Is that early for cutting teeth? She's only four months old," Wyatt said.

"I don't know when they get teeth. I've never been around babies until now. I thought she'd stay little longer than four months," Bridget said.

"Hey, she's not grown and looking at boys yet, so stop moaning about two teeth. Last time I checked, we get a lot more than two in our lifetime. You'll be around for the rest of them." Wyatt was suddenly angry that he would miss all the rest of the things Ella would do. He wouldn't be there when she finally got that chubby belly off the ground and crawled. He'd never see her take her first steps.

"But I'll never see the first two," Bridget said.

"I'm going to move my things back upstairs if you are truly ready to take over her care." Wyatt didn't want to talk about teeth anymore. He wanted to take Ella back from Bridget and put her into her cradle to finish her nap while he did the rest of the morning chores.

The laundry needed to be taken down out of the lobby and put away, along with a few dozen other things.

"Upstairs? Where have you been staying?"

He pointed to the second downstairs bedroom. "Right there."

"In my parents' room? Who gave you permission to sleep in their bed and . . ." She raised her voice.

He pointed a finger at her. "Don't you yell at me. I had to be near you in case you needed me in the night, so *I* gave me permission to sleep in that room. It's just a bedroom, Bridget."

She slapped his finger away. "I'll yell anytime I want. It might be just a bedroom to you, but it's my parents' room to me, and you had no right to sleep in there."

"Good Lord, were they saints or something?"

"I thought they could both walk on water, so don't you belittle them. Just get your things and go back up to your old room. I'll get it cleaned."

"Well, have at it, darlin'. You take care of Ella and clean all my germs out of the sanctuary. I'll be in the basement working on the floor again, since you don't need me for anything else."

"That's exactly where I want you. Out of my sight all day."

"You going to make your own food too?"

"I'm well. I can do anything," she said.

"Then I'll see you at dinner."

"I said I was making my food. Not yours."

"Oh, no. The deal was that I got room and board and

a dollar a day. I've been slighted already for the past week, and since you are well, I'll be in the kitchen for dinner," he said.

Ella began to cry and chew on her fist.

"Shh, don't cry, sweetheart." Bridget's tone softened.

"Her next bottle is already made and in the refrigerator. Heat it to body temperature in the pan that's on the stove. You'll have to boil a kettle of water and let it cool, then make up her next bottles. Half canned milk. Half cool water. One can makes three bottles. She usually has one about every four hours, give or take a few minutes. Good day, Miz O'Shea." He marched into the bedroom where he'd been staying. He opened his trunk and removed every single item belonging to him out of the room, hefted the chest onto his shoulders, and carried it up to a cold room on the second floor.

"Women!" he huffed as he fell onto the bed.

His conscience pricked at him. *Hey, you prayed she wouldn't die, remember? You asked God to spare her so she could raise that little girl baby, and now you are mad because he did and you had to give your toy back, aren't you? If you want one of your own, go find a wife and have a dozen, but don't be angry at God because he answered your prayers.*

"Okay, okay." He conceded defeat and went about setting his things out to make the room his one more time. In two weeks the quarantine would be lifted. He would have been in Huttig a month by then. He'd written his mother a note and left it along with postage money on the porch under a jar for Clark to take to the post office for him. He hoped the child didn't buy penny candy with the money and toss the letter into the nearest ditch. He'd told his mother that he'd be home in six weeks; that he'd decided to spend a few weeks in the small town for rest and recuperation after a year of hard work. Wouldn't she be surprised to see him two weeks early? He would be two weeks early, because Wyatt was leaving one hour after the doctor lifted the quarantine. It would take that long for him to pack and find someone to get his trunk to the train station.

He heard Bridget in the kitchen, but he didn't even peek inside on his way through the lobby and down to the basement. If she was healed and ready to go back to her routine, then far be it from him to butt in and get in her way.

Bridget carried Ella to the kitchen and had to sit while the bottle warmed. Ella fussed and gnawed at her knuckles until her mother finally put the bottle nipple into her mouth. She latched on to it and began to suck, and more tears streamed down Bridget's face. She didn't want to be giving her daughter a bottle; she missed the closeness of nursing. Now it was over after only four months, and she'd never have that feeling again. She would never marry again—that was for sure—so there would be no more children.

She'd overestimated her strength and was so tired by the time she fed Ella, changed her diaper, and rocked her to sleep that she could barely even think of cooking dinner for Wyatt. But she'd drop graveyard dead before she admitted it to him and let him win. He'd already won too blasted many battles. Every four hours, day and night, he'd arrive at her bedside with evil in a bottle and make her take two spoonfuls. He wasn't winning this one.

She was delighted to find an already cooked roast surrounded by potatoes and carrots in the refrigerator when she went looking for something quick to prepare. Lizzy must have sent it over—bless her heart. Bridget heated the oven and put the roast in to warm, made a pan of biscuits, and set the table, alternately working and sitting in five-minute stretches. She was glad Ella had gone to sleep. She couldn't begin to imagine trying to make a meal with the baby hanging on her hipbone.

When the clock in the lobby struck twelve times, she had the table ready for Wyatt and actually looked forward to seeing him, even if she would never admit it aloud. She'd show him that she wasn't a whining little girl but a full grown woman who could claw her way back from death's door.

Wyatt washed his hands and face and combed back his blond hair, which had gotten entirely too long. But how did one get a barber to come to a quarantined hotel? When he went into the dining room, Bridget was waiting for him at a table laid for dinner. He'd been having his meals in the kitchen, standing up mostly, with Ella on his hip.

"This looks very good," he said.

"Don't think with one little compliment you'll erase the errors of your ways," she said.

"We have to spend two weeks together in this place. I don't know about you, but I'm not very happy about it, so let's at least try to get along," he said.

"Or?"

"What do you mean?"

"What if I don't want to get along?"

"Then fight with yourself. I'm not cut out for battle."

"What are you cut out for, Mr. Ferguson?" she asked.

"Right now, eating lunch," he said.

"Ah, so you are from the city."

"What?"

"You have lunch at noon and I bet dinner usually at eight? We have dinner at noon and supper at five in the country."

"You don't live in the country. Pass those biscuits before they get too cold to melt butter," he said.

She handed him the platter of biscuits, followed by a larger one of meat and vegetables. "I do live in the country. Huttig is country. We all eat dinner and supper rather than lunch and dinner."

"Why are you so grouchy today? I figured you'd be happy to get out of that bedroom and be able to hold your baby. Instead you're an old bear with an ingrown toenail and a sore tooth to boot."

"I'm angry. I've never been angry in my whole life

until now, Wyatt. And I don't know what to do with it," she admitted.

"Never?" He frowned.

"Not that I can remember. Oh, there were the sisterly spats when we were kids, and then there were the little fits when my hair wouldn't go up just so for an event, but not this all-consuming, pure old rage that I feel now," she said.

"Not even when your husband was mean?"

She shook her head. "Not even when he . . . disappeared."

Wyatt poured gravy over the potatoes on his plate and pondered. "Did you want to die?" he finally asked.

"God, no. I wanted to live so I can see Ella grow up and so I can see Catherine and Alice again and grow old with my sisters and my daughter around me," she said.

"What happened in the dreams you fussed about when you took the medicine?"

"Most of the time they were nightmares about Ralph," she said.

"Then that's the problem."

"How can that possibly be the problem?" she asked.

"I reckon you lived in so much fear that it blocked out any other emotion. Love. Anger. Passion. Anything that had to do with emotions, because any of those could bring about more anger from him. So fear took over everything inside you. Then Ralph disappeared, and you found out you were having Ella at about the same time.

So you had to plan for her, and motherhood became your all-consuming passion. The anger you should have felt back then is just now coming to the surface. You'll have to deal with it like you did the fear, or it will eat you up."

"That makes sense, but explaining it doesn't make it go away, does it?" she asked.

"No, but love will. Love your child and yourself. Put enough of that into a heart, and there's no room for anger."

"Who died and made you so smart?" she asked.

"No one, thank goodness, and I'm not smart. I just see what your problem is. I expect that a lot of women who get knocked around are angry later that they didn't kill the sorry rascal who was mean to them. It's just a matter of deduction."

"Would you? If you were a woman and someone beat you for not putting the glasses on the dinner table the right distance from the plates, would you want to kill him?" she asked.

"I wouldn't think about it more than a split second. If I were a woman and I'd given my heart to a man, only to have him beat me, I'd kill him without blinking twice. Men who beat women do not deserve to live. *My* wife wouldn't have to kill me; my mother or my dad would do it for her."

Suddenly the black cloud that had surrounded her all day lifted. Sunshine poured into the kitchen through the window, and two doves landed on the sill. Their cooing reminded her of Ella and the noises she liked to make. Bridget actually smiled for the first time in days.

Wyatt saw the smile but didn't say anything. He hoped her dark mood had passed. He surely did not want to live in the same house with an angry woman for two more weeks. If he had to be jailed with Bridget, he'd far rather that she be pleasant.

After dinner she washed up the few dirty dishes and checked on Ella, who had awakened and was busy trying to catch one hand with the other. Bridget picked her up from the cradle and carried her to her room. Cleaning her parents' room could wait until later. Suddenly Wyatt had not committed an unforgivable sin after all. Her mother wouldn't care if he'd slept in her bed. Not one bit, especially in light of the fact that he'd been there because he was caring for Bridget and Ella. The older Ella O'Shea would have given him the bed and slept on the hard floor without a pillow to repay him for all he'd done.

She carried Ella to the kitchen and prepared a bottle. They spent the rest of the afternoon in Bridget's room; Ella playing on the bed behind a barricade of pillows, and Bridget knitting a sweater for Alice's birthday.

Wyatt measured, cut, and hammered boards into place all afternoon. When he ran out of lumber, he almost whined. Now what was he going to do to occupy his time for the next two weeks? He was sitting on a broken-backed chair when he remembered the telephone. He took the stairs two at a time and burst out into the lobby just as Bridget was going to the kitchen.

"I need to make a phone call to the lumberyard," he said.

"They don't have a telephone. They've got one at the Commercial and at the mill, and we have one. I don't know of any others in town," she said.

He grabbed up the phone and asked the operator to put him in touch with the mill, and he went through several people before he got a man who could help him. By the time he hung up, the man had vowed he'd have a porchful of lumber delivered from the yard by noon the next day.

"Why'd you order so much?" Bridget asked.

"You said you wanted the attic done too, and they might balk at coming even up onto the porch of a quarantined house twice," he said.

"Okay," she said amiably, and she went on toward the kitchen.

"You're not going to argue with me?"

"No. I want the job done. I can afford the wood. You get paid the same whether you're doing laundry or building floors. With luck I'll be able to do laundry in a few more days when I get all my strength back. Lying abed makes a person weak," she said.

Was this the same woman who'd argued with him, fired him at least twice a day, and fought over every single issue? He could scarcely believe his ears.

"Need some help in the kitchen? I can't do anything more in the basement or the attic until tomorrow," he said.

"We're having leftovers. You might see about Ella and bring her in if she's awake," Bridget said.

He was speechless. Bridget trusted him to hold the baby. Would wonders never cease?

He found Ella beyond a mountain of pillows with her eyes barely open. She smiled brightly when she saw him, and he could have sworn she reached out her arms. She was wet, so he changed her from the skin out—a new diaper and gown. Then he hugged her close, inhaling the sweet baby smell.

And for the first time in a week he thought about Ilene.

"Well, I'll be damned," he swore under his breath. For someone he thought he absolutely could not live without, he'd sure forgotten about her quickly in the face of losing Bridget and worrying about Ella's catching the deadly flu bug.

His chest didn't even try to wring blood from his heart at the mental picture of Ilene with her dark hair and soulful eyes. He was still in awe of such a change of heart when he heard someone pound on the hotel door and then footsteps running away. He pulled back the lace curtain to find no one and nothing there. Probably just a prank, he thought, until something fluttered in his peripheral vision. He opened the door a crack to find a bundle of mail tied with a piece of twine and Clark waving from the yard next door.

He stuck his hand out far enough to wave and pick up the bundle without letting the cold wind whipping across the porch touch Ella. He recognized his mother's handwriting on the top letter, but before he could pull it out, Bridget was behind him, eyes glistening in anticipation.

"Letters! Maybe I've got something from Catherine or Alice." She reached for the mail.

He handed her the whole bunch and waited.

"One for you. My, oh, my, what lovely stationery. Do you have a sweetheart somewhere, Wyatt?" Her heart spasmed into a knot. She could hardly wait for the quarantine to be lifted so she could send him on his way, so why did she care if a rich lady wrote him letters on fancy stationery?

"I said I wasn't married. I didn't say I didn't have someone," he said.

Now, why did you do that? he asked himself. *Ilene is the only woman in your life, and you can't even have her, so why are you claiming to have a sweetheart somewhere?*

"Well, here's your letter from her. I hope it has the best of news. How about we sit here in the lobby and read our mail before supper? I, for one, wouldn't enjoy a bite of food knowing there was news from my sisters." She sat down on the settee and promptly opened the letter from Catherine.

Wyatt followed suit, sitting on the other end with Ella in his lap. He carefully opened the cream-colored envelope and unfolded the two-page letter. His mother was very worried about him, and he was to find a phone and call her the moment he received the letter so she'd know what exactly he was doing in a little southern sawmill town in Arkansas. His two older brothers were fine. Clayton was dating Elvina Poteet, and things were looking promising. Ilene and Harry had broken their engagement. The story was that it was amicable, but she'd heard from a reliable source that Ilene had been caught with another young man in a very compromising situation. Harry was lucky he'd found out before the marriage. The weather in Alvord was cold, but they hadn't had snow, and his father was eager for him to come home. There was going to be a family discussion about an office job for him instead of so much travel. It was signed, *Love, Mother.*

He tucked it into the bib pocket of his overalls to read again before he went to sleep. Ilene was no longer engaged, at least not to his best friend. Now, that opened up a whole new world.

He looked across the settee at Bridget, who was smiling at something in Catherine's letter, then down at Ella, who'd leaned forward and was trying to chew a gallus button off his overalls. Suddenly Ilene seemed far away and not nearly so important.

Chapter Nine

Bridget pulled back the curtains in her bedroom, hoping for sunlight, only to find a gray sky above and dense fog swirling and rising from the ground. For a moment she saw the past in the fog and the future in the sky. Nothing was black or white. No definite right, no sinful wrong. Just shades of gray, and she didn't like it.

For the past year she'd kept her emotions—other than loving her daughter and sisters—in complete check. Vowing she'd never trust another man hadn't been difficult until the past week, but every day it got more so. Wyatt worked all day without complaining, in the basement until it was finished and the past two days in the attic. He whistled. He played with Ella. He didn't grumble about the quarantine. He even helped with the dishes after supper, and the previous night he had entertained her all evening by reading the first two chapters of *The Adventures of Tom Sawyer* aloud. Who would have thought a boy's book could be so amusing?

Without wanting to or even knowing when it happened, she trusted Wyatt Ferguson. And every other day, as regular as clockwork, there was a letter on that fancy stationery. She'd hear the knock on the door and find the small bundle on the porch. She'd read her mail, lay his letter on the clerk's counter, and give it dirty looks every time she passed by. Just the day before she'd figured out that not only was it expensive linen-textured writing material, it also smelled good. She would swear on her mother's grave—and that was holy ground— that it had been handled by a woman wearing Muscade from Jerome. Her mother would wear it on special occasions, and Bridget could recognize the scent anywhere.

She dropped the curtains and meandered out into the lobby, where the laundry hung waiting to be taken down and folded. Wyatt's idea of doing it at night was ingenious.

Wyatt startled her when he pushed through the sheets. "Good morning," he said cheerily.

"What's so good about it?"

"Well, you are alive. We've got another week of quarantine down, and there's just one more to go. The attic floor is a third of the way done. I built a nice fire in the fireplace to chase the fog doldrums away," he said.

"Quit being nice. I'm not in the mood for nice," she said.

"Want a good, rousing fight to get your blood boiling, do you?"

Bridget's face went as gray as the fog and sky.

"Hey, I didn't mean a knock-down, drag-out type fight. I meant a good argument," Wyatt said.

"No, I don't want an argument," she lied.

He grinned and searched for something near and dear to her heart that they could fight about to bring her up out of the blues. "I think those manly pants you wear are abominable. You look so much better in a dress. I expect that when Ella is old enough, you're going to put them on her too. And I bet you won't even let her cut her hair like all the other girls will be doing by then. By the time she's old enough to make up her own mind, she's going to want one of those bob things." He waved a hand around his head.

Bridget bristled. "What I wear or do not wear isn't a bit of your business, Wyatt Ferguson. I happen to like my overalls. They're not men's pants. They were made for a woman and look feminine, and if Ella wants to wear them, I'll see to it that she has a closetful. But she's not cutting her hair. No sir. I don't care if all the little girls in the whole county have that ugly, cut-off stuff; she isn't going to wear her hair like that. She'll have braids until she is old enough to put it up, just like I did."

"What if I say she can have a bob?" he asked.

"You won't be around to have a say," she answered.

"Who knows? Fate might deal a hand, and I'll be stuck in Huttig on some job or other for a long time.

Since I've been holed up in this hotel with ya'll for all this time, it could be that Ella and I will become very good friends, and she'll want my advice on matters like her hair."

Bridget propped her hands on her hips. "You'll be out of here so fast that you'll catch your coattails on fire with the speed."

"And what makes you think that?"

"All those fancy letters." Bridget wished she could take back the words the moment they were out of her mouth.

He grinned. "Are you jealous?"

She knotted her hands into fists to keep from slapping the smile off his face.

"Of what?" she said through clenched teeth.

"Why, of my letters, of course. You aren't getting any fancy notes from anyone, are you? Just plain old letters from your sisters, who no doubt are tickled to hear back that you are alive and as cantankerous as ever."

"I'm not cantankerous. A woman can be blue in ugly weather without being called cantankerous."

"Yes, you are cantankerous. You came in here picking a fight, and now you've got it, and you're even worse than in the beginning," he said.

She narrowed her eyes. "I am not."

"Yes, you are. You ever heard of fight or flight?"

She shook her head.

"For years you were in the flight mode. You ran from anything that meant feeling. Now you've discovered the fight mode, and, like a little child, you want to try it out and see if it feels as good as you'd always imagined."

"I am not a little child," she said.

"That's all you picked up on from what I said? I'm going to work. I don't have time to stand here and argue with a little girl."

"You are abominable."

"Maybe, but I speak the truth. What'd you do with Ralph's body?" he asked abruptly.

It was on the end of her tongue to spit out the very place they'd used their three shovels to dig the hole and bury the man. She caught it just in time. "Go to work. I'm tired of fighting with you."

"Almost had you, didn't I? I almost did what Quincy couldn't do in months. Did he ever try to make you so mad that you'd forget yourself and spit out what he wanted to hear?"

She glared at him.

"I think I worked you up out of your depression, so I'll go to work in the attic now. You can thank me by making a chocolate pie for lunch."

"I'll put arsenic in it," she said.

"Then feed my piece to the rat."

She looked around in all the corners. "What rat?"

"The one that I have to kill before I finish my job at the Black Swan," he said.

She made another quick scan to make sure he didn't really see a rat.

"You through fighting now? Did I win?"

"In your dreams. I won."

"I think I did." He chuckled.

"Confinement is driving you crazy."

"Yes, ma'am, it could be. Know what happens after a couple fights all morning?"

She clamped her mouth shut. She knew what would have happened if she'd fought with her ex-husband all morning. For one thing, it wouldn't have lasted that long. One cross word and she'd have been picking herself up out of a corner of the room.

Wyatt crossed the room in two easy strides and scooped her up into his arms. With her feet dangling, he kissed her soundly on the lips, tasting black coffee and cinnamon from her breakfast toast. Then he sat her back down.

"That's what happens when a couple has a big old fight. They make up, and that makes it all worthwhile. See you at lunch. And the fancy letters are from my mother."

He left whistling a snappy little tune.

Her breath caught somewhere in her chest, and every nerve tingled. She reached up to touch her burning lips, only to find them as cool as a chilled cucumber. Her mind raced almost as fast as her heart, and she was sure for a moment that she heard church bells ringing off in the distance.

Wyatt sat down for several moments on the attic steps. He'd been cocky in starting the fight and ending it that way, and it had come back to bite him on the hind end. His head was reeling and his heart pounding. He was glad for a few minutes to regroup and recoup from that kiss. Who would have thought that Bridget O'Shea could send him into a tailspin like that?

Red-haired women had never appealed to him, and he'd never had one of those things for short women like some men did. Those who needed a dainty little lady to make them look and feel big and strong.

Stupid! It's not the outside, even though she is a very lovely lady. It's what's inside. She's a remarkable woman. Like a rose that's coming out of the bud and blooming, she's going to be astounding when the blossom is full blown. So if you are in the remotest way possibly liking what you see, you'd best be doing something about it.

"I am," he whispered. "I'm running away as fast as these two legs can carry me."

He climbed the rest of the way up to the attic, picked up a board, measured it, and reached for the saw. He'd work hard and not argue with her again. The making up was too tough on the nerves.

Bridget dropped a glass and had to clean up the mess. She burned a pan of coconut cream filling for a pie; be damned if she'd make chocolate after that remark he'd made. And she wasn't going to thank him either. Sure enough, he'd stirred her up out of her depression, but he didn't deserve a pie. She would have worked her way out of the blues without that fight.

A ray of sunlight crept through the lace curtains, throwing a motley pattern onto the floor. Ella reached up from the pallet on the floor and tried to catch the dust motes in the rays. Bridget sat down on a kitchen chair and watched her for several minutes.

Is that what Alice and Catherine were talking about that embarrassing day when they wanted to gossip about being married? Does Quincy make Catherine's knees go all weak when he kisses her, like Wyatt did mine? I can't imagine Ira making Alice swoon, but he must, because she gets that look in her eyes when she talks about him. I can't feel like this about Wyatt Ferguson. I simply cannot.

"Something isn't right, Ella. Not only is it not right, it's terribly wrong. Why would he be out looking for sawmill work when his mother is rich enough to write him letters on fancy paper like she does? Oh, my dear God."

She threw her hands over her mouth.

Wyatt Ferguson was an investigator.

The Contiellos' had sent him to find Ralph. That's what was really going on. Those letters weren't from his mother; they were from Ralph's. Looking back, Bridget was sure that she'd seen that same stationery on Mrs. Contiello's desk. She'd been so stupid, playing right into his hands. He'd probably been planning to set up shop at the Commercial while he investigated her. She'd given him the perfect ruse when she hired him to kill a rat.

"What do I do now? It has to be the way things are. Why else would he ask me about Ralph right in the

middle of a fight? Oh, Ella, what am I going to do?"
She began to wring a dishtowel into mere threads.

The baby gave her a big two-toothed grin and kept
reaching for dust motes.

Dinner was awkward, eaten in silence. Supper wasn't
much better. After Wyatt helped Bridget with the dishes
and the day's laundry, she went to her quarters and shut
the door with him outside. He went upstairs to read the
next few chapters of *Tom Sawyer.* It wasn't nearly as
humorous without an audience.

He washed up a little after eight and was propped
up on pillows set against the oak headboard when he
heard someone climbing the stairs. That one step always
creaked when any weight was put upon it. He'd have to
check it for dry rot before he left the next week.

He wondered what Bridget would need from the second floor of the hotel but decided it wasn't his business
if she wanted to prowl around at night. Maybe there
was a book in storage in one of the other rooms, or else
she wanted to be sure he'd brought down all the dirty
towels from the guest bathrooms.

A weak knock on the door set his heart into second
gear. She would never knock on his bedroom door without an emergency. He grabbed his overalls and pulled
them on, barely taking time to hook the galluses before
throwing the door open.

"This is the hardest thing I've ever done," she said.

"What is it? Is Ella all right? She doesn't have fever

after all this time, does she? Answer me, Bridget. I don't give a damn if it's not socially proper for you to knock on my door." His talk was fast and furious.

She held a hand up to stop him. "Ella is fine. She doesn't have a fever. And I don't care right now what is socially proper."

"Then what makes this the hardest thing you've ever done?" He leaned against the doorjamb for support. Lord, she was lovely in her gown and wrapper of pure white cotton flannel. Her braids hung below her waist, with a few strands of hair escaping to fluff around her face. Her bare toes peeked out from the hem of the gown, and she'd started wringing her hands again, proving that she was nervous.

"Can you please join me in the lobby? I'm not comfortable standing here with you."

"Why?"

"Because I am . . . because . . . just join me in the lobby. Why do you always make things so difficult?"

"Do I?"

She exhaled loudly.

"Okay. I'll be there in a minute. Do I need shoes? Are you about to throw me out in spite of the quarantine?"

"If I throw you out, I'll give you an hour to pack." She left him to wonder what bug had snuck down her craw.

He found her sitting on a settee, knees drawn up and toes covered. He chose a chair a few feet away and made himself comfortable.

"I want the truth, no matter what it is," she said.

"Okay. Is this about my mother's letters?"

"Partly. But more than that. Just promise me you'll be truthful. I couldn't bear it if you lied."

"Why?"

"Because I trust you," she said simply.

That pricked his heart to the core.

"I'm going to ask the questions, and I want answers. I hate the way we were so uncomfortable at dinner and supper. I thought I could just live with this thing until you left, but I can't. If it's going to keep happening every few months, I have to know now."

"What?"

She came closer at that moment to betraying her sisters than she ever had. She wanted to simply get the whole story off her chest and out into the open, but she couldn't. "How familiar are you with the Contiello family?"

"I met them once in passing in El Dorado. Then I saw the woman at the café with you that day."

"Did they hire you to find their son? Is that why you are really here in Huttig? Was it just a stroke of luck that sent me to the station to offer you a job that day?"

"No, ma'am. And you can trust that that is the absolute truth. I don't really give a damn what happened to Ralph Contiello. I was serious that day when I said he should be shot. I wasn't just blowing smoke to cover up an investigation."

Her eyes were wide and frightened. "Look me in the eyes and tell me that you aren't a detective."

He stood up, took two steps, and kneeled in front of her. He cupped her face in his hands and stared directly into her eyes. Green eyes meeting aqua ones, neither blinking. Both hearts beating a little too fast. His hands burning from the touch of her delicate face. Her face on fire from the contact of his hands.

"I am not a detective. I was not hired by the Contiello family. I'm not here to find Ralph or his body. I don't care. That's the truth."

She gently removed his hands. It was either that or forget society and lean forward and kiss him until his upper lip matched the lower one.

"I believe you," she said.

He went back to his chair. "So now I can stay?"

She fidgeted with the lace on her wrapper. "The letters from your mother? Tell me about them."

"That's pretty personal, but okay, here goes. My younger brother fancies himself in love. My best friend broke up with his fiancée because she found another man. Her name is Ilene, and . . ." He took a deep breath. "In for a dime, in for a dollar. I'm here because of Ilene."

"Your best friend's fiancée?"

"That's right. She's a lovely woman. Tall. Dark hair that flows to her waist and beyond. Big brown eyes. I met her after she was engaged to my friend and fell in love with her on the spot."

Bridget's heart dropped somewhere down into the basement. Maybe there were other men in the world who'd turn her inside out with a simple kiss, but she doubted it.

"I see. But why does that put you here?"

"I was on my way home to Alvord, Texas. The wedding was to be in six weeks, and I was dreading being there for all the parties surrounding a marriage. Having to be in the same room with Ilene and see her in love with Harry. I didn't think I could stand it, but I didn't have anywhere to go—until you needed a rat killed. The rest you know," he said.

"So now that she's available, you'll go to Alvord and tell her how you feel?"

"I don't think so. If she'd throw Harry over, how could I trust her? And how does someone build any kind of relationship on a shaky foundation? I'd always wonder if she'd run off and leave me," he said.

"I'm sorry," she said.

"I'm not. I found out I was in love with what I wanted her to be. I saw pretty and figured it was more than skin deep. I was wrong."

"Takes a big man to say that," she conceded.

"Thank you. We finished?"

She thought about it for a few minutes, then slowly shook her head. Like he said, in for a dime, in for a dollar. She might as well have it all, even if it wrecked her world even worse.

"Tell me about that fancy stationery. It doesn't come from a family that's dirt poor and looking for work at a sawmill."

"I never said I was dirt poor or looking for work at the sawmill."

"You did too. You said . . . oh!" She slapped her fingers across her mouth.

"Yes, that's right. You said I might as well not apply at the sawmill because they were cutting back, and you said I could work for you for a dollar a day and room and board. I just took the job so I didn't have to go home. I never said I needed the money."

"And then . . ." she said through her fingers.

"And then you got the flu, and we got quarantined."

"I'm sorry," she said.

"I'm not. I got a lot of things worked out in the past weeks. I might not stay once the quarantine is lifted, so you'd best be thinking about hiring someone local to do your handyman work and kill your rats."

"Your father doesn't really own a general store?"

"I didn't lie. My great-grandfather Ferguson—an Irishman, I might add—started out with a general store. That would be before the Civil War. He raised my granddad in the store, and when it came time for Gramps to take over, the store was making good money, so he built another store. That first one was up in northern Texas. Gramps and his wife, Granny Sarah, had eight boys, so when they came of age, Gramps sent them off in different directions to manage a store each for the family. My father went to Alvord. He married my mother, who was quite wealthy in her own right, and they've diversified. Railroads. Farming. Ranching. We are into oil now and doing quite well. That's where I met the Contiello couple that one time. I was at a dinner looking for investors as well as new land to lease for drilling."

She was embarrassed but, even more so, angry all over again and mostly at herself. "Why didn't you just say so in the beginning?"

Stable as water, her conscience reminded her. *You jumped to a conclusion about his seeking mill work.*

Yes, well, I found a man to help me. I didn't say he had to be dirt poor, did I? she argued right back.

He shrugged. "You didn't ask."

"Your mother probably thinks you've landed in an insane asylum."

"No, but she probably will when I go home and hit her with the news that I've found the place where I want to put down roots," he said.

What his mother thought wasn't up for discussion that evening. He wasn't about to tell Bridget that he'd answered more questions on paper than he ever had before, and they all had to do with a strawberry blond lady with a baby. The first time he used the phone and called his mother, he was careful not to say anything that could be carried back to backyard-fence gossip club. That left the letter avenue, and his mother, Dorothy Wyatt Ferguson, had used it, threatening to call if he didn't answer her letters promptly.

Bridget was appalled. Looking at herself from Wyatt's mother's point of view was scary as hell.

"Where's that?" Bridget held her breath and waited for the answer.

"Over by Healdton, Oklahoma. There's a big oil boom going on, but that little place has promise. My friend, Briar Nelson, owns the Rose Oil Company and lives there now. Met a woman and married her. I visited them a few weeks ago. I'm going to try to convince my folks to put a permanent office in Healdton. We'll run our oil production out of it, and I'll take care of it."

"I see," she said softly.

"My mother wanted to come to Huttig by train to see the Black Swan."

"She did not. You are lying." Bridget's tone changed immediately.

"Yes, I am. See there? You can tell the difference between a lie and the truth, Miz O'Shea. Don't underestimate yourself. Is that all for tonight?"

"I think it is. Thank you for being honest," she said.

"I'm just glad you're not kicking me out into the cold in my bare feet," he teased.

She giggled.

He thought it was the sweetest sound in the world. Even prettier than tickling the rim of crystal stemware with Champagne in it. Even prettier than Ilene combing her hair in the dusk.

Where did that come from? he asked himself. There was nothing that beautiful. Or was there?

Suddenly he didn't want to go up to his lonely room.

"Want me to go get *Tom Sawyer* and pick up where we left off last night?"

She nodded. "I really would like that. He's stolen my heart. There might be hope for boy children after all."

"You mean you doubted that?"

"Yes, I did. Lately I've thought that boys were only slightly higher life forms than common house mold," she said.

"My lord, how did you ever say yes to a proposal?"

"That is a puzzle, isn't it?"

Chapter Ten

By the beginning of the third week of quarantine Wyatt and Bridget pretended the kiss had never happened. It brought about dreams they never talked about and emotions they worked hard to suppress. They'd finally settled into a routine not unlike one of married people. Breakfast, dinner, and supper together. Laundry before they went to bed. Wyatt pitching in to help with Ella and the supper dishes. Bridget getting her strength back and looking forward to listening to Wyatt read chapters of *The Adventures of Tom Sawyer* at night.

The doctor said he would arrive sometime in the middle of the morning on Tuesday, so Bridget kept an ear trained toward the door as she made a chocolate cream pie for dinner. She was well; she hadn't had any fever in days. Maybe he'd lift the quarantine a few days early. That idea stopped not only her thinking process but her hands as well. The pie dough lay on the worktable in a perfect circle, and she stared at it like a fortune-teller looking into a crystal ball.

Did she really want Wyatt to leave the Black Swan? She needed to decide in the next few minutes, because if she wanted him to go, she should do nothing but let nature take its course. If she wanted him to stay, she needed to suddenly feel a weakness coming on and pretend to be sick again.

She still hadn't decided when she heard the front door open. *Honest.* She had to be honest because she'd made a vow the night Ralph died that if she could stay out of jail and raise her child, she would never lie again. She wiped her hands on her apron and went to the lobby to talk to the doctor.

Wyatt made sure Ella was sleeping soundly in her cradle before going to the basement to check the furnace. Several days before he'd started dragging the cradle into the lobby during the day to save Bridget steps back and forth to the bedroom. The baby was almost ready for a crib. Wyatt made a mental note to bring down the one he'd seen in the attic. The springs on the bottom had a little rust in places, so he'd need to scrub that away, but the iron scrollwork was in pristine condition.

He'd dreaded the three weeks of jail time he thought he'd been sentenced to the day the doctor had diagnosed Bridget with the flu. In retrospect it had gone by rapidly. Two weeks had passed. The doctor was due any minute, and Wyatt hoped he didn't lift the quarantine a week early. He'd told Bridget he was leaving when he could, but suddenly he had trouble thinking about walking out of the Black Swan. The idea of leaving Ella caused a lump in his throat; it grew larger when he thought of telling Bridget good-bye.

He was halfway up the basement stairs when he heard the front door open. The doctor had arrived. Whether he left tomorrow or a week from then would be decided in the next few minutes. Suddenly he wished he could turn back the clock just one day and better prepare himself for the good-byes ahead of him. A week or a day? Either was going to be very painful.

He took the steps two at a time and shut the door at the top of the stairs behind him. When he reached the lobby, he looked across the room to find Bridget coming from the kitchen. She wore an apron over her overalls. Flour was smeared across her forehead, and she was frowning. His gaze followed hers to the doorway where the doctor should be standing.

Ilene Randolph looked from one person to the other. The red-haired hired cook really shouldn't wear such dowdy clothing. She should wear a white uniform or a pristine apron over skirt and blouse. Perhaps a red or blue tie at the neck. What hotel would let its cook wear black and white checked overalls?

Then her eyes settled on Wyatt in his faded overalls

and patched shirt. He needed a haircut, and he had dirt on his chin. What in the world had her precious Wyatt gotten himself into?

The scenario froze in place for a long, pregnant moment, and the door opened behind Ilene. She turned to see a man with a black bag in one hand and a scowl on his face.

"What the devil is going on here? I told you both that no one was to come in or out for three weeks. I don't care that Bridget feels better. Rules are rules," he said.

"She wasn't invited. She just pushed right in the front door," Bridget said. The woman was dressed in the latest fashion. A lovely charcoal wool coat over a black suit and the cutest little hat atop her jet black hair. Her eyes were dark chocolate, her skin like half milk and half coffee. Smooth yet slightly toasted.

The doctor shot the intruder a look meant to fry her on the spot. No sane person walked right past two quarantine signs and into a flu-invested hotel. "Can't you read?"

"Yes, I can read, but that doesn't mean I can't do exactly what I want. I came to see Wyatt, and I'll see him no matter what the signs say. I'll speak my mind and then be on my way," she said.

"Too late for that," the doctor said. "This place is under quarantine for the next week. You disobeyed the signs, so you're in here for a week."

The woman looked around frantically. Laundry hanging in the lobby. A baby starting to whine in a cradle. The cook staring dumbly. Wyatt not rushing to her side.

"You are crazy. I'm leaving right now."

"I am the doctor in this town, young lady. You should have paid attention to my signs. I trust that's your bag you dropped on the porch? I'll kick it inside when I leave."

"You can't make me stay," she protested.

"I can, I will, and I am. If you try to leave this place before the week is up, I'll have the sheriff put you in jail. Huttig is not going to suffer another epidemic like we had last year. That's why I'm putting the full quarantine into effect here," he said.

"Wyatt, make him let me leave," she said.

"I'm sorry. I can't make him do anything. Why did you come to Huttig anyway?" Wyatt asked.

She teared up and rushed across the room, throwing herself dramatically into his arms. "I had to see you. I simply had to talk to you before I . . . well, before I tell Arty I'll marry him. I had to talk to you. I saw the way you looked at me."

"Well, while they sort out their love life, Bridget, let's check you out," the doctor said.

Bridget followed him through the open door into her living quarters.

He pointed to the sofa. "Sit there, and I'll have a listen to your chest and back. I see that you've been getting back into your usual routine."

She strained her hearing toward the lobby, where Ilene's voice rose an octave. She could understand the tone but not the words. "I'm fully back into my routine and ready to open the doors for business."

"Started going over everything with soap yet?"

"When you say I can, we will," she said.

"You've got a pretty good little laundry set up here. Why don't you go ahead and strip everything down, wash it, and put it back on the beds. I believe the danger has passed for you to spread anything, but as a precaution, I'm keeping you shut in for another week."

"Can you please let that woman leave?" Bridget asked.

He held up a finger and fixed the stethoscope into his ears, listened to her heart and lungs, both front and back, and took her temperature. "No, can't help you there. She should have listened. Put her to work on the laundry."

A wide grin split Bridget's face, and her eyes twinkled. "Now, that's an idea."

"One more week and you can take down the signs. I'm not coming back unless you need me," the doctor said. "Make the best of it, missy. It could be a long week."

"I believe it could be," Bridget said with a sigh.

She sat still for a few moments after the doctor left. So that was Ilene, and she'd come for a final chance at Wyatt Ferguson. She was a pretty thing for sure, and Bridget could see where a man like Wyatt would be attracted to her exotic looks. But Bridget couldn't hide from the woman forever, so she headed toward the lobby.

The sight that greeted her brought on a giggle. There

stood Ilene, rigid as an iron bedpost, coat still on, arms crossed across her chest, sparks flying from her eyes, and her foot tapping. Wyatt was busy changing Ella's diaper and putting a fresh gown on her and apparently ignoring the grown princess in the middle of the floor.

"How can you live in this squalor, Wyatt Ferguson? And changing a baby? What is going on here?" she demanded.

"What is going on here? Well, I took a job working for this lady. A dollar a day and room and board, and I intend to see it out to the end. You should've paid attention to the signs out front before you barged in here. There's a telephone. You could have called. How did you know where to find me anyway?"

"Reuben said you were in a little town in Arkansas called Huttig. I had no idea you were in a flu-infested hovel. Have you lost your mind?" Ilene asked.

"No, actually I think I've found it. I've had a lot of time to think, and that's why I took the job to begin with."

Ilene glared at Bridget. "Take my bags up to my room, and make me some tea. I think I feel a headache coming on."

"I hope to hell not," Bridget swore. "There's seven empty rooms up there. Wyatt has one. You take your choice of the rest. The hotel is closed for another week, so neither Wyatt nor I will be waiting on you. As a matter of fact, I'll hire you too. A dollar a day and room and board, just like Wyatt gets. I need help cleaning all the rooms and getting this place ready to open in a week."

"You are more insane than he is. I do not do common labor. I'm not a maid, and I won't do anything while I'm here," she said.

"Wyatt, call the sheriff up in El Dorado and tell him to send a car for Miss Randolph. If she doesn't have any intention of working, then she's of no use to us. She can sit out the week in the county jail for all I care," Bridget said.

Ilene pointed at him. "Don't you dare."

"Your choice. I didn't ask you to barge into the hotel. The only way you stay is if you work," Bridget said.

"I'll stay, and I won't work. You can't throw me out, and I don't have to do one thing," Ilene said.

Wyatt bit the inside of his lip. Evidently he'd taught Bridget well in the art of arguing. She had held her own with Ilene, and although he felt more than a little sorry for the Texas lady, he was very proud of his Bridget.

His Bridget!

Good Lord in heaven above, where did that thought spring from? She certainly was not *his* Bridget. They were barely friends making the best of a terrible situation. One kiss did not make her belong to him by any means.

"I can and will throw you out," Bridget said to Ilene. "This is my hotel, and I make the decisions. I'd love to throw you out in fact. It would make my day and week a whole lot more pleasant. I don't want you here, and I wouldn't have a single second's worth of guilt if I called the sheriff and had you quarantined in his jail. So are you working in my quarantined hotel or sitting in his jail? You've got one minute to make up your mind. That's how long it'll take me to get to the phone."

Bridget didn't run, but she didn't walk slowly. She sincerely hoped Ilene kept her mouth shut, because she would far rather have a women who looked like her in jail than next door to Wyatt.

What does it matter to you who's next door to him? she asked herself as she lifted the phone from under the counter and picked up the receiver.

"Okay, okay, don't call. I'll work."

"Good, I can use the help. Take your bags up to your room, and change into something you won't ruin by working," Bridget said.

"I don't have anything like that," Ilene said. "Maybe I could just sit behind the counter and take messages?"

"That would be boring and not worth your room and board, much less a dollar a day. You look to be about my sister, Alice's, size. She left a pair of overalls here. You can work in them."

Ilene wrinkled her nose but was wise enough to keep her mouth shut. She'd show Wyatt she was more than fluff and powder. He'd insinuated that when they'd argued. She must have misread him a few months ago when she saw him admiring her from afar. That was unusual for her; she could usually tell what a man was thinking thirty seconds before the thought entered his head. She could have sworn he was in love with her, and he was so much more handsome than his best friend,

Harry. She'd had a vision of the two of them walking out of a church—they'd make such a lovely bride and groom—and she had begun to manipulate the situation so she could have him.

First she flirted with Arty until he begged her to leave Harry. That was a necessary step—to put one man between her and Harry—but it was just a pathway to Wyatt. Once she and Arty broke up, then Wyatt wouldn't feel as if he'd betrayed a friend by admitting he'd been in love with her all the time. Where on earth had her plan gone wrong?

She picked up her bags and shot him a pleading look that he ignored. Ilene Randolph never failed when it came to getting what she wanted, and she wouldn't this time either. She had a whole week to work her wiles. Maybe this wasn't a bad thing but a good one. There wasn't a man alive who could outrun her when she set her mind to have him, and she was holed up with Wyatt Ferguson in a situation where he couldn't run.

The room wasn't as bad as she'd figured it would be. It looked comfortable if rather plain, with a quilt over the sheets on an oak bed. At least there was a modern bathroom at the end of the hallway. She couldn't imagine what kind of work she'd do in a shut-down hotel for the next week.

"Here's your new uniform," Bridget said from the open doorway.

"Do you really own this place? All by yourself?"

"I do. My sisters and I ran it until they married, and now it's mine, so I'm your boss. When you've changed, you may start in the room nearest the bathroom. Strip the beds, take down the curtains, and remove all the doilies. We'll wash them and put them on the line in the lobby. They'll be dry by bedtime, and we'll put our normal laundry on for the night as usual."

"You're not serious," Ilene said.

"Why wouldn't I be serious?"

"Laundry? My hands will be ruined."

Bridget held up her hands and examined them. "Maybe, but you'll have lots of time to make them pretty again after the week is done."

Ilene sat down in the rocking chair. She'd pass the time of day looking out the window. She was not doing laundry. That's what servants did.

"Send it out."

"Can't. Remember that quarantine sign that you couldn't read? Can't send out germs."

"I can read," Ilene protested.

"Good. You want me to write down your chores for each day?" Bridget said.

"You're in love with my Wyatt. That's why you're being so mean to me. Well, honey, let me tell you something. He won't have you. He's rich as a king, and his momma would die before she'd let him bring someone like you into the family," Ilene said.

Bridget turned to walk out the room. "It's not a matter

of his having me. I wouldn't have him. I had one man and divorced him. Why would I want another one? Get dressed, and start earning your pay."

Divorced? Well, praise God, now I know I can trap him by the end of the week. He wouldn't be foolish enough to fall for a divorced woman. The Ferguson family would disown him if he set his eyes on a divorcée.

"I'll expect that first load of laundry down in the kitchen in fifteen minutes," Bridget said.

Wyatt had escaped to the attic. He'd finished putting the flooring down, but his excuse was that he had to pull the stored items out of the corners and put them back where they belonged. He fully intended that the job would take him right up to the dinner hour and perhaps half the afternoon.

Ilene huffed and puffed, hoping that Wyatt would come to her rescue to help with the heavy load she toted down the steps. But he was nowhere to be seen. Probably that slave-driving woman had sent him into exile in another part of the hotel far away so she wouldn't have a chance at him. That was fine with Ilene. She didn't want him to see her in such dowdy clothing. She'd just as soon only see him at the dinner table; by then she'd be all beautiful in her finery, her face touched up and hair fixed. Or maybe she'd "accidentally" make a mistake and go into his room wearing that new bright red dressing gown with the lace.

When she reached the bottom of the stairs, Bridget held that squalling baby on one hip and had a big grin on her face. Ilene could have thrown the kid out into the yard to freeze to death. She would never ruin her body with a pregnancy, even if she did like children, which she did not. And that *NOT* was in capital letters. If Wyatt insisted upon children, she would allow him to adopt one or two, but only if they came with a nanny.

"What are you grinning about?" she asked rudely.

"We don't usually carry the laundry down. It's too much work. We just toss it from the top step and then pick it up at the bottom."

"You could have told me that before now," Ilene grumbled.

"You've just learned lesson one. I'm making dinner. Do you know anything about running a washing machine?"

Ilene shook her head. "We have paid help in my house."

"Which is where?"

"Chico, Texas."

"Must be rich," Bridget said.

"Enough that I don't have to work," she said.

"Then this will be another good lesson. Momma said we all had to learn to run the hotel, so we started with chores when we were very small. Pick up the clothes, and I'll teach you to do laundry," Bridget said.

"I'll never use the lesson, so it won't be any good at all," Ilene said.

"Yes, you will. Someday when you are older and wiser, you'll remember the lessons you learned this week and be grateful for them," Bridget said. The moment the words escaped her mouth, she believed them for the first time. If she'd never endured that year with Ralph, she would never appreciate a good man. If she'd never had fear in her life, she wouldn't know the wonderful peace she had now.

Ilene literally snorted. It sounded strange coming from a proper lady.

Bridget led the way to the kitchen. "I've got water boiling on the stove and cold water running into the washer. While the first load runs, you can take a bucket of water up to the first room and wipe down everything. When you are done with that, use the water to mop the floor."

"Good God, I'm to be a charwoman?"

"You are to be whatever I tell you. After this room is scrubbed down and the linens on the line, dinner should be ready. Then you can help me with the cleanup and have a half-hour break while I put the baby down for a nap."

"Where's her father?"

"Pushin' up daisies somewhere, I hope," Bridget said.

She instructed Ilene in the finer points of sorting linens, showed her how to get the first wash load running, then sent her with a bucket of hot, soapy water and a rag up to the guest room. Ella had just begun to sit up alone, so Bridget threw a pallet down on the opposite side of the kitchen from the washing machine. She propped pillows around Ella and went back to preparing smothered steak in the oven, mashed potatoes, hot rolls, and corn. The pudding for the two pies had cooled, so she filled the waiting cooked shells.

It took Ilene twice as long as it would have taken Bridget, but then, the girl had no training. Bridget made a mental note right then to be sure that Ella didn't grow up spoiled and ignorant. She said a silent thanks to her mother for all she'd taught her daughters.

Several strands of Ilene's hair had come down to stick to the sweat on her forehead. She didn't look quite as proper, but nothing could mar her beauty. Wyatt would be a fool not to admire her.

Wyatt spent part of the morning staring out the attic window at the backyard. The sun was bright, and the pine trees stood tall and majestic, their evergreen leaves belying the fact that winter still had a few weeks left before spring pushed it into the history pages. The garden would need turning over before long, and the shed out back could use a coat of paint. But that was someone else's job, not his. He'd be long gone before spring wrapped her warm arms around Huttig, Arkansas.

His grumbling stomach told him dinnertime was approaching, and he dreaded sitting at the same table with Ilene and Bridget. The argument that had ensued after Bridget and the doctor left the lobby had not been pretty. When he'd pushed Ilene back out of his arms, her eyes went mean and hateful, and she'd accused him of toying with her affections, flirting when she was engaged to his best friend, walking around all moony-eyed when she and Harry were in his presence. And then she'd declared that the only reason he was holed up in such squalid conditions was because he was running from his own feelings for her.

He'd lied without blinking when he told her she had imagined everything and should not have come to Huttig. Everything that she said had been right on the money, true as a plumb line—once. But in the weeks he'd been at the Black Swan, he'd realized he wasn't in love with Ilene but with the *idea* of being in love. That alone was childish and immature. Harry deserved more than Ilene, and he sure didn't deserve a friend who avoided him because he was jealous.

Bridget yelled up the stairway that he had five minutes. He slowly headed toward the second-floor bathroom to wash up. It was going to be one long, long week.

The clotheslines were filled in the lobby, so he had to push sheets aside to walk in. He could smell fresh bread, and his mouth watered—at least until he found the women waiting at the table. Then his appetite failed. He sat down and began to load his plate, passing the serving dishes to his right, brushing Bridget's hand and sending sparks dancing around the room. Taking dishes from Ilene on his left and feeling nothing. One woman had traveled miles and miles by train to seduce him—the very woman he had once ached for—and he could care less. The one who never wanted a husband was the one who'd gotten under his skin. Was he one of those men who only wanted what they could not have?

"This is too heavy for my taste, but I suppose a week of country food won't spoil my figure or my looks, will it, Wyatt?" Ilene said. Her voice was soft and low with a heavy Texas drawl that usually drove men into a frenzy.

"Bridget has quite a reputation as a good cook. You should see this dining room when it's open for business. I've seen it full up and people waiting in the lobby for empty chairs," he said.

"I'm sure people from a small town like this would think it was very good cuisine, but I'm also sure none of them has dined in Paris or London, have they?" she said.

Bridget gave Ella a small bite of potato. She pushed it out of her mouth with her tongue, and Bridget pushed it back in.

Ilene shuddered. "Do you have to do that at the dinner table? Children should never sit at the table with adults. They should stay in their rooms until they are old enough to behave properly."

Bridget bit the inside of her cheek to keep from telling the lady to go to *her* room because women did not chase men across three states. Ladies waited for men to come courting; they didn't take courting to them.

"Ella has always joined me at the table. She sits on my knee, where she belongs. Paris and London might have different rules, but that's the way we do things in a small town. Here, have another helping of potatoes.

You've got a long afternoon of work ahead of you. You might get faint if you don't eat enough."

"Wyatt darlin', did I tell you that I danced with your older brother, Reuben, last week at a party your mother hosted? He's quite the gentleman," Ilene said.

Wyatt's blood ran cold. It looked as if Ilene was determined to dip her hands into the Ferguson wealth with one son or the other.

"And how was dear old brother Reuben, and how did you leave Mother? She writes often and keeps me up on the news, but is she all right? Looking well?" Wyatt asked.

"Oh, they're all just fine. You know your mother. Always so prim and proper. She had the party catered by that new restaurant in Dallas. It was quite the talk of the town, I'm here to tell you."

"Who did you go with? Or did Mother invite you?"

"Arty invited me. Reuben invited him and told him to bring a guest. I was the guest, but you know how much I enjoy the parties at your folks' mansion. Such a lovely place in the middle of little ol' Texas," she said.

Bridget felt as if she were back in third grade, when Iva Ruth Simmons goaded her about not having a real house but living in a hotel. There had been a school yard fight, and Bridget wound up with a black eye, but Iva Ruth had a bloody nose, so Bridget figured it was about even. That day, sitting in the Black Swan, listening to Ilene, she didn't figure anything was even. The other woman had a definite edge. She knew Wyatt's family. She was beautiful and well traveled.

Bridget had been to Marion, Louisiana, once or twice and to El Dorado a few times. But what did it matter? She argued with herself silently. No one would ever know that she'd learned to trust Wyatt Ferguson. If he wanted to make a fool out of himself, then he could step right up to the plate and show the world, Paris and London included, that all it took to turn a man into an idiot was a woman with a silver tongue and a little determination.

Wyatt finished off his dinner and reached for the chocolate pie. "Bridget, you are awfully quiet. Why don't you give Ilene a lesson on Huttig? Tell her about your family coming here and building the Black Swan when the town was just beginning."

"I'm sure it would bore her. She's so well traveled for such a young lady, and Huttig is just a small town," Bridget said coolly.

"I'm not that young—not that a woman tells her age you know—but, Wyatt, old darlin' that he is, happens to know that I'm the same age as his younger brother, and that would be twenty-one. And, yes, I am well traveled. Papa said a girl should be well rounded, so he hired a chaperone and sent me to Europe to study for a year. I'd have stayed longer, but the war got in the way. So how old are you? Thirty?"

The dig failed to dent Bridget. Most days she felt

every day of thirty, even older during the year she was married.

Wyatt raised an eyebrow. "So?"

"Twenty on my next birthday," Bridget said honestly. After all, she could not lie, since God had been gracious enough to let her get away with "the incident," as she'd come to think of it.

"And that is when?" Wyatt asked.

"March twenty-seventh."

"You're only nineteen, and you're divorced? Oh, my, but you ruined your life early on, didn't you?" Ilene said.

"All depends on how you look at it. Some would say I ruined it. I say I learned a lot, so it isn't ruined. I suppose it's time to get all this cleaned up so we can move on to scrubbing the lobby floor and fireplace this afternoon. Wyatt, did I tell you the doctor said I could begin cleaning and open the doors one week from today?"

He shook his head.

"He did, and Ilene has arrived at just the right time. Where will you be working this afternoon?" she asked him.

"In either the basement or the attic, but if you need me for anything, just holler up or down the stairs," he said.

"You mean you'd scrub floors?" Ilene's eyes widened.

"It all pays the same. A dollar a day. And after that first week of learning how to take care of Ella, anything is easy. You know, babies ought to come with an instruction manual for menfolk. It comes natural for women, but it's hard going for daddies."

"She's not yours, so don't be calling yourself a daddy," Ilene said.

Wyatt winked at Bridget on his way out of the dining room. "She was one day in El Dorado."

"What's he talking about?" Ilene said.

"It's just something that happened when we were in El Dorado. Meant nothing, but it did show me that all men are not created equal, like folks sometimes say."

Chapter Eleven

"*E*verything *happens for a reason.*"

That's what Bridget's mother said often when everything was topsy-turvy in the world. She had named Bridget for water, and most of the time Bridget had the qualities of water. Ever moving. Taking the path of least resistance. But then there were other qualities too. Water was life giving, and a person could see through it. She remembered her mother's telling her once when she was very small that she had given her a special gift along with her name. When Bridget asked what it was, her mother had smiled and said there would come a day when she would need it, and on that day it would be revealed.

Bridget rocked Ella to sleep and thought about that day.

She looked up toward the ceiling in her bedroom. "Just anytime you want to toss that gift down here would be fine. I could use some special powers to understand this whole mess. The past three days have about undone me, and there's four more to go. What possible reason could there be to endure Ilene's whining and insults? What did I do wrong?"

As if the answer fell from heaven, Bridget understood. Ilene had been sent to Huttig to irritate her, and in her irritation Bridget would think less and less of Wyatt and look forward with anticipation of instead of regret to his leaving. Not seeing Wyatt every day would be a small price to pay for not having to ever be in Ilene's presence again.

Her mind went on to explore why Wyatt had been sent to Huttig in the first place, because if she'd never met him, then she wouldn't have to deal with Ilene. He'd thought he was in love with the woman, so he was sent to put time and space between him and the situation to clear his head.

"So the rat was just a pawn in a complicated chess game?" she asked.

"Everything happens for a reason," her mother's voice whispered over her right shoulder so distinctly that Bridget whipped her head around to see if someone was there.

With her new deductive powers she went on to wonder why fate had thrown so many mistakes into her life. The puzzle pieces began to fit snugly together and make perfect sense. Words could not describe it, but in her heart she saw the past and understood how one "why" fit into the slot with another "why". And understanding washed away the bitterness and replaced it with wonder.

"This, too, shall pass."

Another of her mother's adages came to mind.

"Can you make it pass a little faster?" She looked up. There was no answer for that one.

Wyatt laced his hands behind his head. His head was barely an inch from the headboard; his feet would dangle over the footboard if he stretched out to his full length, but he'd drawn his knees up. Moonbeams flowed through the lacy curtains, making patterns on the blanket across his knees. For a while he let the different designs entertain him. There was Ella's hand as she reached for the dust motes that showed up in the air when the sun's rays flowed into the kitchen. Her fingers were all splayed out and trying to gather up the sunbeams the way a fairy would gather dust for a bit of magic. Then there was the shape of a long strawberry blond braid like Bridget's when she was sick.

Someday, maybe when he was eighty, he'd look back on this experience with fondness, but that night it was irritating. Until then he'd never realized what a predicament he would be leaving Bridget in when he departed. She already had the worst reputation of anyone in Huttig. Married. Husband missing. Divorced. Baby born with her mother's maiden name. All before she was twenty. Now she'd be marked with another scarlet letter. She'd lived in the hotel for three weeks with a man. Mabel would tell everyone who would stand still and listen that Bridget was doubly ruined. A woman simply did not live with a man, not even in a hotel under quarantine, without a chaperone.

A smile tickled the corners of his mouth. Bridget would do fine. She was a strong woman who didn't give a hoot about what people thought. If she did, she never would have divorced her husband after he went missing. She would have taken the easy way out and passed herself off as a widow lady. The sickness had even fried all the fear from her eyes, and she could stand her ground in any argument. Even one with the notorious gossip, Mabel.

For a moment he wondered why on earth he'd wound up in Huttig, Arkansas, in this predicament, but a few minutes of reflection assured him that he'd brought it on himself. He hadn't wanted to be in the same company with Ilene and the whole wedding party thing, so he'd let himself be coerced into a job he didn't need or want. He had learned valuable lessons while he was doing that job, though. Even though he'd done some carpentry work with the hired hands as a teenager when his father was adamant that he and his brothers learn to do something useful during their summer months, he'd never been given a whole job, not any without supervision. Finishing the floor in the basement and putting one in the attic might not be such a big thing, but it was fulfilling that Bridget had trusted him to do it.

Then there was the matter of his heart. He examined that avenue while the light of the moon drifted through the curtains and made Ella's profile on the blanket.

Even Ilene's appearing like a blast from a wild Texas tornado was a good thing, if he could get past her whining and long sighs. Living with her for even three days was taxing; he couldn't imagine a lifetime of it.

Bridget was a much different matter.

"Life is what you make it."

His father's words came back to haunt him. Wyatt nodded in agreement. Bridget had taken life by the horns and made it pleasant. Wyatt was blessed to have known her.

Ilene was tired to the bone and bored to distraction. The past three days had lasted longer than eternity. She could scarcely imagine the next four. They couldn't go by fast enough to suit her. Wyatt had avoided her since that first argument, making sure that the hotel owner, Bridget, was in attendance anytime she talked to him.

Well, the witch was downstairs with that slobbering brat of hers now, wasn't she? And there were no other guests in what passed for a hotel. Good Lord, the house in Chico where Ilene grew up was twice as big as the Black Swan, and they called it home, not a hotel.

She sat on the bed, pillows behind her, the idea of sneaking across the hallway into Wyatt's room exciting her more and more. Finally she pushed back the covers, opened her luggage, and removed a red silk kimono. Her feet hit the cold floor, and she was tempted to put on slippers, but bare feet were so enticing. She wrapped the robe around her and tied it very loosely, undid the top three buttons of her silk nightgown, and eased the door open.

The downstairs witch probably knew every single squeak of the floorboards and would come running with a midnight chore if she heard anything. Ilene thought of the braid down her back and stopped long enough to undo it and fluff all her black hair around her shoulders. Hair down. Feet bare. Buttons undone to show the top of her breasts. Anything else? She pondered for a moment and shook her head.

Wyatt's stomach growled, and he remembered the remains of a peach cobbler in the refrigerator. He pushed back the covers and pulled on overalls over his derby ribbed long underwear. He was halfway down the stairs when he heard Ilene's door open. He stopped and looked up.

She fairly floated across the hallway, long hair flowing down her back, tiny feet shining in the moonlight coming from the open door behind her. She looked like a dark-haired angel, and she was headed straight for his room.

He cleared his throat at about the same time she reached the other side of the hall, and she looked down.

"Wyatt darlin', I couldn't sleep and thought we might talk," she whispered from the top of the banister.

Wyatt wasn't totally stupid. One cry of ruined reputation by Ilene Randolph and he'd be standing in front of a judge. He shuddered at the very thought that just weeks before would have sent him into pure ecstasy.

"In my room, at this time of night?"

"No one is here. Who would know?"

"I'm hungry. I was about to go to the kitchen for some peach cobbler. You want to talk, you can join me there. I'd advise you put on some shoes or socks. The floor is cold," he said.

She watched him disappear behind the full clotheslines and stomped her foot so hard, it ached. That Bridget O'Shea was an Irish witch. She'd put a spell on Wyatt and probably had caused him to be hungry at that very moment so he'd be out of his room.

Ilene buttoned up her nightgown, pulled the kimono tightly around her slim body, and marched down the steps. Her bare feet might be the very straw she needed to break the witch's spell. She'd talk for a while, then declare that her feet had gone to sleep from the cold. Would Wyatt please carry her back up to her bed? If she could get him that close, she'd have him at the altar in exactly four days.

What had begun as running away from Arty had now become a game of mind and will. Ilene would win. She always did. She'd never wanted something and not gotten it. From the time she laid eyes on Harry's best friend,

Wyatt, she'd wanted him. She was engaged to Harry at the time, so it was requiring a lot of manipulation and planning, but she'd have Wyatt Ferguson—one way or the other. And it had nothing to do with all those lovely Ferguson dollars. The Randolph dollars were just as impressive. Joining the two families would create a fantastic Texas empire. In a nutshell, Ilene mused as she pushed aside the laundry, she wanted Wyatt, and showing that Irish witch that she could best her was simply the frosting on the wedding cake.

Bridget heard Wyatt heading for the kitchen and smiled over the top of her knitting. That tall Texan did have an appetite and a bottomless sweet tooth. It wasn't anything unusual at all to put half a pie or cake into the refrigerator after supper, only to find it gone come breakfast time. At least he was faithful in cleaning up the mess he made. She wouldn't abide dirty dishes in the sink. That was just asking for rats to come into the house.

She put Ella into the crib Wyatt had brought down from the attic the day before and set up right next to Bridget's bed, gave her a kiss on the forehead, and headed for the kitchen. She'd mentally marked a piece of that leftover cobbler for her own nighttime snack. She could already taste thick yellow top cream poured over a chunk of cobbler.

The lobby was dark except for the light drifting in the windows, but she could make her way from her bedroom to the kitchen or any other room in the hotel without even a little moonlight. She'd been raised there and knew every nook and cranny, every single place a piece of furniture stood. Yellow light seeped under the kitchen door in small streaks on the dining room floor.

She heard Wyatt saying something in that tone that he used when he was suppressing anger. Surely the quarantine hadn't made him so stir-crazy that he'd started talking to himself. Maybe the flu had finally awakened and attacked him? She remembered how she'd mumbled and fought her demons while trying to recover from the flu.

She swung the door open to find Wyatt sitting at the worktable and Ilene leaning seductively across it, whispering something to him.

Lord, she'd never felt so dowdy in her life. There was Ilene in red silk, looking like a siren out of mythology, and Bridget in her faded blue striped dressing robe with a tear in the collar. But there she was, and to stammer and stumble around would look much worse than just plowing right into the room.

"So ya'll got hungry too, did you?" Bridget asked.

"Yes, I did. The cobbler was calling out to me. Come and sit with us and have a piece. I even got out the cream. Figured you'd be protecting your part. Though I was half hoping you'd forget so I could have all of it," Wyatt said.

He talked a little too fast, and his smile was plastered on, as if he was being very still for a photograph. He wasn't fooling Bridget one bit. He was every bit as jumpy as a holiness preacher sitting on a barbed-wire fence in hell.

"Don't mind if I do. How much do you want?" Bridget looked at Ilene.

"Not a bit. I didn't come in here to eat," she said icily.

"Couldn't sleep, could you? Want to start another load of clothes and hang them over the chairs in the dining room?" Bridget asked.

Ilene rolled her dark eyes toward the ceiling. "Don't you ever think of anything but making me work? I came to the kitchen so Wyatt and I could have a private conversation, so if you'll take your pie and go on back to your room, I would appreciate it."

Wyatt looked like a caged raccoon. Bridget's first notion was to leave him to get out of the trap without her help, but then she remembered all the work he'd done, plus the fact that he'd taken care of her during the illness. She supposed she did owe him one small favor.

"I think I'll stay here. You dressed like that—why, if someone were to look in the window and see you here with Wyatt, they might think I was running one of them bawdy houses. This hotel has had a good reputation since the day my papa built it, so I don't think I want to ruin it. Now, if I'm in here with you two, then if someone should look in the window, they'd know nothing was going on," Bridget said.

"How can we have a private conversation if you are here?" Ilene asked.

"I'll just shut my ears and concentrate on chewing

this cobbler. You sure you don't want some? It's really good with cream on top," Bridget said.

Poor Wyatt didn't have sisters and had no idea how subtle a good girl fight could get. From the undertones he grasped, there was more going on than Bridget's coming or going. A war was being fought right under his nose, and at that very moment he hoped Ilene lost.

Ilene spoke to Wyatt but glared at Bridget. "I told you, I'm not eating that greasy pie. But if you must stay, then stay. Wyatt, I told you that that first day I met you, I fell in love with you and couldn't marry your friend. We need to talk about it."

"Why? I told you that I don't love you, and I haven't changed my mind in a couple of days, Ilene. I hope you told everyone that you were taking one of your trips and not that you were coming here to tell me that bit of news. I suppose it'll be embarrassing if you did when we go home."

"You'll sing a different tune when we are out of this hovel and back in our own environment. You loved me then. I could see it in your eyes." She hoped her words were barbs that stung Bridget's heart and soul.

"I was infatuated by you. You are, after all, a lovely woman, but I did not love you. And you don't love me, Ilene. You didn't love Harry enough to marry him, and I became a means to the end."

Bridget spooned out another helping of cobbler and added cream. Wyatt eyed the cobbler bowl and reached out to take another portion for himself. Ilene could have slapped both of them until they were blue.

"How can you say that to me?" Ilene pouted.

"Because it's the truth, probably," Bridget said.

"You stay out of this. I told you it was a private conversation. You aren't invited to talk. So sit there and be quiet," Ilene snapped.

"Honey, this is my hotel. You are my employee. So you don't get the right to tell me to be quiet. If you don't want to hear me talk in my own kitchen, you can finish your week out in a jail cell in El Dorado," Bridget said.

Ilene pointed a long, tapered finger at Bridget. "Stop threatening me."

"Stop acting like a child. And that was not a threat. It was a promise. Grow up. Wyatt doesn't love you. You don't love him. You just don't want to lose the fight. It'd be a miserable life between you if you did win, so think about that," Bridget said.

"What makes you say that?" Wyatt ran his fingers through his blond hair.

Ilene pushed her long black hair away from her face. "I'll like to hear that answer too. Have you got a crystal ball in your witch's bag that can tell you we'd be miserable together?"

"To begin with, I'm not a witch, Ilene. Never was much good at hiding what I'm thinking, but I'm not a witch. I don't know why I can see that you two wouldn't make a good couple. It's just something I feel."

"Then you feel wrong," Ilene said.

"Okay, then maybe you'll understand this. Wyatt, how many kids do you want?"

"A whole houseful. I loved growing up with four brothers. I loved the big family and all the fun. In fact, I'm afraid I've fallen in love with Ella. It's going to be hard to tell her good-bye. She won't remember me, but I'll always remember her."

"Ilene?" Bridget asked.

"None. I never want children and have no intention of doing that to my body. The minute you have a baby, you are old. Look at you. Not even twenty, and your life is over," Ilene answered.

"I do appreciate honesty, but this isn't about me; it's about you and Wyatt. Don't you think that will be a bone of contention between you? He wants lots of kids, and you don't want to have any," Bridget said.

"How many would you have?" Ilene shot back at her.

"Oh, I think at least three, and I'd hope they were all girls, since I was so happy growing up with two sisters, but I don't suppose I'll ever have another one, since I'd have to have a husband, and that's out of the question," Bridget said.

"Wyatt can have twenty kids if he wants them. We'll adopt. There are orphans everywhere who need a good home. We can hire a nanny or two, and everyone will see us as good parents to the unfortunate," Ilene said.

"You an only child?" Bridget asked.

"I have an older sister in south Texas."

"She have children?"

"Lord, no. She's married, but she doesn't intend to have children."

"Interesting. Your father and mother, with all that wealth, are going to leave it to a bunch of orphans you've adopted. The Randolph name and money in hands like that?"

Ilene pondered that for a while. Her father would never leave his fortune to anyone but blood. She'd be cut out of his will, and the Randolph money would go to a cousin before it went to a passel of adopted children.

"Maybe I'd consent to one child."

"Remember now, it's going to make you look old," Bridget said.

"I'll simply have to work at not letting it do that to me. We'll hire a wonderful wet nurse and nanny, right, Wyatt?"

He didn't answer.

"Now, where are you going to live? Wyatt told me he's a notion to move to Healdton, Oklahoma, and run the oil office for his father's firm. It's a boomtown. Scarcely enough housing. Lots of riffraff coming in and out to work the new oil wells. I heard there's a section over there they call Ragtown because of all the tents that've been thrown up for living quarters. There's very little social life there. You going with him?" Bridget asked.

"He can come home on weekends and holidays," Ilene said. Her nose wrinkled at the very idea of living in a boomtown. She'd seen them when the trains went through; she would not live in such conditions.

"You going to trust him around all those hussies who follow boomtowns? The ones who dress like you are to-night and look at him with dollar signs in their eyes? He might be tempted to stray with no children at home to keep him focused on his wife and family."

"I'm not that kind of person," Wyatt said defensively.

"How does anyone know what kind of person they are until they're suddenly confronted with great adversity or prosperity? Ilene has always had prosperity, and she's not done too badly in adversity. She can do laundry fairly well now, and today she made near perfect gravy. But I don't think you can truthfully say what you'd do until the time comes. So I'm not a witch, but I'm also not blind. You two would be miserable together."

Ilene went to the cabinet. She took down a small bowl and a spoon and returned to the table.

"Give me some cobbler, and put extra cream on top. You're right. Thinking about all that leaves a nasty taste in my mouth, so I'm eating cobbler to erase it. We would have looked really good together at the parties, Wyatt."

"Yes, ma'am, we would have," he said.

"Your Greek god blond looks and my exotic dark ones would have made every head turn," she said.

"Looking good and living miserably," Bridget said.

Ilene looked right at Wyatt. "It isn't worth it, is it?"

"No, it is not," he said.

"Okay, then this is the story we're going to tell. I was

afraid I was making a rebound mistake with Arty, and I went to my sister's for a week to think. She wasn't home, but I stayed in her house. Her servants will vouch for me or she'll fire them. If you ever breathe a word of what happened here, I'll kill you myself," she said.

"And bury him in the garden? Want me to help you?" Bridget giggled.

Wyatt jerked his head up. "Was that what you did?"

"There are three shovels in the toolshed. When the quarantine is lifted, you can take your pick of the three and get about digging up the garden if you think Ralph is in there. It needs a good spading. Hasn't been done since Quincy turned it over for us last spring. If you find Ralph, be sure to get in touch with the Contiellos. They'll want to claim his body and find out who killed their son," she said.

"What are you talking about?" Ilene asked.

"It's a private conversation." Bridget grinned.

Chapter Twelve

*T*hree more days.

That was Bridget's first thought when she awoke that morning. Just three more days, and the ordeal would be over. Wyatt could go home, and routine would heal her raw nerves. Ilene would definitely be out of her hair and hotel, and Allie Mae would be back, which would be a tremendous blessing.

They had four of the rooms cleaned and ready for guests, should any be brave enough to stay in the hotel after a quarantine. That left two more, and then she and Allie Mae would take care of the two Ilene and Wyatt had occupied. She mentally organized her days. On Tuesday she could reopen the restaurant, so she'd need to put in an order for pot roast, carrots, and potatoes and extra cans of peaches from the general store. That should be done on Monday. Then Monday afternoon she would make the pound cakes so they'd be ready to slice.

Routine, plain and simple. She craved it as she had strawberries when she was expecting Ella. When she had it she'd be satisfied with her life again and stop thinking about things that couldn't be.

Three more days.

That was Wyatt's first thought when he opened his eyes that morning. Saturday, Sunday, and Monday. On Tuesday morning he and Ilene would leave. She'd go her way at the train station, and he'd go his. That alone was symbolic, and he was glad she'd brazened her way through the quarantine, because now he had closed the book on that chapter of his life.

In the past month Wyatt felt as if he had truly grown up. At twenty-five, he had accepted job responsibility and been an asset to the family's many businesses, mainly since the oil boom. But the past few weeks had given him time for introspection. Arguing with Bridget, helping her to overcome her own fears. He felt he would be leaving Huttig knowing himself much better than he did the day he was hired to kill a rat.

The aroma of coffee and bacon wafted up the stairs and into his room. Bridget was already in the kitchen making breakfast. He grinned and threw off the covers, pulled on his work clothes, and headed to the basement to take care of the furnace.

Three more days.

Ilene held up three fingers. That's how much longer the nightmare would last before it ended. She intended to put the whole experience so far back in the attic of her mind that she never thought of it again. She would never, ever, not in her lifetime, break the law, be it stealing, cheating, or even speeding in her new automobile. One week in a jail called the Black Swan had definitely broken her from sucking eggs.

She smiled at that idea. When she'd been a little girl, they had a big, round cook named Pearl who often used that phrase. When Ilene got into trouble, Pearl would ask her if the experience had broken her from sucking eggs.

Ilene didn't understand it until Pearl explained. Farm dogs often snuck into the henhouse and sucked the eggs. Folks broke them by putting red-hot pepper on the eggs. Ilene fully understood what Pearl was talking about when she looked at her three fingers. She'd been broken from sucking eggs, and the pepper had burned badly.

She tossed back the covers and slipped into the work overalls that had belonged to Bridget's sister. She viewed them as prison garb, and after three days she would never wear something so ugly or coarse again. When she had her shoes tied, she went into one of the "unclean" guest rooms, gathered up the bedding, doilies, and curtains, and tossed them down the stairs.

The bacon and coffee smelled wonderful, but she could have that any morning without the chain-gang labor that went along with it.

"Good morning," Bridget said when Wyatt and Ilene arrived within seconds of each other.

Wyatt went straight for Ella and picked her up from the pallet in the corner. "Smells good in here. Rest of the place should be warmed up in a few minutes. I got a good fire going. Looks like we're going to have a beautiful sunny day. And how's the sweetheart this morning? Hungry for bacon? Well, we'll have to ask Mommy about that. She says you're too young for anything but oatmeal for breakfast."

"Don't you go putting all the blame on me, Wyatt Ferguson. She only has two teeth. Besides, bacon is too greasy for her digestive system. She's only four months old," Bridget said.

Ilene ignored them both and pulled plates from the cabinet to set the table. She had never known what a fool Wyatt was over children. In her wildest imagination she could not see herself feeding oatmeal to a slobbering four-month-old child. She had to avert her eyes at every meal when Bridget started putting food into that kid's mouth.

"Well, don't you worry, Miss Ella O'Shea. Time will

come when you can have bacon and coffee both," Wyatt said.

"No coffee until she's past thirteen. It will turn her toenails black," Ilene said, then wished she could take the words back. She had no intention of talking about Ella or even acknowledging her presence.

"My Papa told me that," Bridget said.

"And my dad told me the same thing." Wyatt grinned.

They both looked at Ilene.

She shrugged. "Pearl. Our cook told me. She was just full of homely wisdom."

Bridget finished frying bacon and dumped a dozen beaten eggs into sizzling butter in a separate skillet. While they cooked, she pulled biscuits from the oven and transferred them to a napkin-lined basket.

"When did you drink your first coffee?" Bridget asked Ilene.

"When I was about five. I wanted to see what black toenails looked like," she said.

"I was ten. My older two brothers had started having a cup with their breakfast, and their toenails looked just fine," Wyatt said.

They looked at Bridget.

"I still don't drink it. Prefer tea. Had nothing to do with toenails. First time I tried it, I asked Momma for sugar and cream, and she told me if I was going to drink coffee, I had to take it the way it came out of the pot. Her theory was, life didn't come with sugar and cream, and you had to take what you got handed. It was a lesson I didn't learn too well until I was much older."

Ilene put two heaping spoons of sugar into her cup of coffee and added an inch of heavy cream. "Are you going to make Ella drink it black?"

"Yes, ma'am, I am," Bridget said. "Give me that baby, and have your breakfast, Wyatt. I'm sure you've found a dozen things to keep you busy these next three days."

He handed Ella across to Bridget. "I found a high chair in the attic. It needs some cleaning, but I think she's about ready to sit in it. It would free you up to eat with two hands."

"Then bring it down," Bridget said.

"I'll make it my first order of business this morning. Pass the butter please," Wyatt said.

"You two ever fight?" Ilene asked.

They both broke out into laughter.

"Is that no or yes?"

"That would be yes. You just hit the hotel on four good days. Until you arrived, we fought about everything," Bridget said.

Wyatt pondered on that for a while. Surely they'd had one rousing argument since Ilene had arrived. But not a one came to mind. Maybe that was because since Ilene had barged into the hotel, he'd kept his distance from both women. Arguments couldn't happen without contact.

Ilene's dark eyebrows knitted into a solid line across

her forehead. "You mean you used to argue, my arrival put an end to it? Wonder what that means?"

"Probably that now I've got you to argue with, I'm giving Wyatt a rest. Doesn't that make you wish these next three days would get on past?" Bridget said.

"You'll never know how much," Ilene murmured, and she kept her eyes away from Ella pushing oatmeal back out onto her chin.

After the morning meal Ilene began her laundry duties. Wyatt headed for the attic to find the high chair. Bridget made a meatloaf and stirred up a chocolate cake for dinner and supper.

Why hadn't they fought? Bridget wondered, then realized quite suddenly that she was afraid to argue with Wyatt. He'd said that after an argument a couple made up, and she was sure she couldn't stand another of those passionate kisses. Already she had dreams about his taking her into his arms and kissing her. In one dream they were on a beach, with the sound and smell of the ocean all around them. In another they'd been on the top of a high mountain, with cool air blowing against their faces as he put his hands on her cheeks and kissed her. Then, in a third, they'd been in a tent in a desert, oppressive heat swirling around them, and he'd looked deeply into her eyes and kissed her.

That was the reason she'd been so careful not to fight with Wyatt. She couldn't endure his leaving if he kissed her again. Simply trusting him had required a tremendous step. Watching him leave was going to drain every emotion from her body and soul. She'd never known or understood what love was until she met Wyatt.

"Love?" she mumbled. *I am not in love with Wyatt Ferguson. I can't be in love with him, because I vowed I would never fall in love again. So if I am, then I will quite simply fall out of love. I can't do it again. I just can't.*

Wyatt pushed open the kitchen door. "High chair for the princess coming through."

"Just put it over there," Bridget said.

"You look as if you could chew up railroad spikes. Ilene make you mad again?"

"No, she's working out pretty good, considering her upbringing. She's in the lobby hanging up clothes. Didn't you see her?"

He picked up Ella and set her in the white wooden high chair. "No. She's not in there now. Must have gone upstairs for something, and I missed her."

Ella studied her new surroundings seriously, touching the tray and finally figuring out she could pound it with her fists.

"So what put that look on your face?" Wyatt asked.

"That, sir, is none of your business. Thank you for the high chair. Looks as if she's going to like it," Bridget said.

Go away. I need to think about not liking you and certainly not loving you. It's difficult enough when you are in the hotel but near impossible when you are right in front of me.

"Penny for your thoughts," he said.

"Two cups of flour, two cups of sugar in a bowl. Melt half a pound of butter in a pot. Add five tablespoons of cocoa powder and a cup of water. Pour that into the flour and sugar and stir well. Add two eggs, half a cup of buttermilk, and a teaspoon of soda," she said.

"Bridget O'Shea, you do not lie well." He whistled as he left the room.

"But I only need to do it for three more days, and then I can set about getting over you. Out of sight, out of mind. I can do this. I've gotten over much worse things," she muttered.

Ilene came into the room carrying an empty wicker basket. "Who are you talking to? You'd better get an old belt and strap Ella into that chair. She's about to slip out under the bottom of the tray."

Bridget left the cake and rushed to save Ella from a nasty fall.

"You could've taken care of that," she told Ilene.

"Not my job. I get paid a dollar a day, which, by the way, I do intend to collect when I leave here. That is to do laundry and clean. Taking care of a kid is not my job. I didn't birth her, and I dang sure don't want to touch her," Ilene said.

"Testy, ain't we?" Bridget said.

"Just stating a fact. I hope that is chocolate cake you are making over there. Pearl used to make it once a week. I could hardly wait until Sunday after church," she said.

"What's so wrong with Ella that you can't even touch

her to keep her from hurting herself?" Bridget asked coldly.

"Nothing is wrong with her that about fifteen years won't cure. Tell you what. When she's sixteen, you bring her down to Chico, and I'll give her a big debutante party. We'll dress her in a white lace gown and pearls. She won't be slobbering all over everything and using diapers by then."

"Well, how sweet of you. But the answer is no thank you. Once you are out of my hotel, I'd just as soon not see you again."

"Feeling is mutual. I was just stating facts again. I hate babies. They are messy and demanding. I like children when they are about ten fairly well. They can be fun in small doses. At sixteen girls are interested in clothes and looking pretty. That's when I can relate to them. I'm going to hang these up and take a bucket of water up to wash down the room."

"But it takes a baby to make a fun girl later on," Bridget said.

"You raise the baby. I'll take her when she's a little older," Ilene said.

Bridget clamped her mouth shut. She'd make sure Ella was never around Ilene when she was older. That woman would poison a monk's attitude.

Just three more days and she'd be rid of both of them. In ten years she wouldn't even remember Ilene and her smart mouth. She'd always remember Wyatt, but he'd just be a handsome man who'd flitted through her life. *Everything happens for a reason.* Once upon a time he'd been sent to the Black Swan to help take care of Ella while Bridget was sick with the flu. Unlike the fairy tales, where the ending had something to do with happily ever after, he was not a prince but merely a man.

One you let into your heart.

"Yes, and one I removed from my heart when I realized what damage he could do," she whispered to Ella.

"Talking to yourself?" Wyatt asked from the doorway.

"I thought you were going to the attic."

"I came back to tell you to strap Ella in so she wouldn't fall out the bottom under the tray. I meant to do it, but I forgot," he said.

"I can take care of my child. I managed before you came along, and I expect I'll keep on managing after you are gone."

He stuck a finger into the chocolate mixture on the stove and pulled it out in a hurry. "You are spoiling for a fight, Bridget."

"Good Lord, don't you have a lick of sense? That's hot," she said.

"I love hot chocolate," he declared.

"You have rocks for brains."

"I disagree."

She looked up at his smiling face and was mesmerized as it came closer and closer, finally brushing a kiss across her lips. Her body was electrified with sparks, and she wanted it to never end. Just one more moment to put in her memory bank for those times when she was an old woman and had no one or nothing around her.

He broke away and kept grinning. "I told you that when we argue, we have to make up."

She was tempted to wipe the kiss away with the back of a hand but couldn't make herself do it. "You are a rotten rogue."

"Yes, I am." He left, humming a jaunty tune.

Ilene came into the kitchen as he left. "So, what's going on in here? Wyatt is humming, and you are angry. What happened?"

Bridget completely ignored the question and pointed to the stove. "Stir that chocolate, and don't let it scorch."

"I think you lost a fight," Ilene said.

"If it scorches, your cake will be ruined."

"I think you don't like to lose fights."

"I think you've got mush for brains." Bridget smiled.

Chapter Thirteen

Tuesday arrived too fast and yet finally. The part of Bridget that wanted the quarantine to be over so she could at least sit on her porch even if it was cold was glad that it was finally over. That other part that dreaded seeing Wyatt leave was a different matter. That part wanted her to hide in her bedroom and not come out to the lobby to say a proper good-bye that morning.

But adults didn't behave like that, and saying good-bye would finalize the love/hate relationship she had with Wyatt Ferguson. So she put on a day dress of aqua cotton that morning after breakfast and got ready for yet another difficult day.

She'd thought nothing could be tougher than the day she watched Catherine head off for the train station. The three sisters had sat up most of the night over several pots of tea and dozens of cookies discussing the fact that Catherine needed to go get Quincy out of her mind or put him there permanently.

Bridget knew that day six months ago that her sister would never come back to help run the Black Swan again. It was written all over Catherine that she was in love with Quincy. Then, the same thing happened with Alice. Ira went home to Grace, Mississippi, and Alice was miserable. She said she was just going for a visit, but Bridget knew better.

Those were difficult days, but that cold February morning, Bridget faced another good-bye, and it seemed even harder. Wyatt was in his room packing. Ilene was doing the same. Their train out of Huttig left at nine o'clock. Allie Mae would arrive at any moment to begin her work again. Orville had been summoned to drive Wyatt and Ilene to the station. Everything was on schedule and moving smoothly.

At eight-thirty Allie Mae poked her head inside the door and yelled for Bridget.

Bridget carried Ella out into the lobby, and Allie Mae reached for her. "Oh, my, just look how she's grown these three weeks. And two new teeth. Who'd've thought such a short time could bring about such changes? You seen any more of that rat?"

Bridget shook her head. "Orville with you?"

"He's out there. I told him to take down the quarantine signs and bring the car on around to the front. Miss Bridget, you think you could hire him to take Wyatt's place? He's been laid off at the Commercial," Allie Mae said.

"I think that's a wonderful idea. He any good at killing rats?"

Allie Mae snuggled her face down into Ella's hair. "I believe he could do about anything for a job. We'd like to get married come June, but we got to have money. She smells so good, and I just love a baby's hair, don't you?"

"Oh, my God. A girl with babies on her brain," Ilene said from the bottom of the steps.

"Is this the fancy lady?" Allie Mae asked.

Ilene smiled brightly.

"Fancy lady?" Bridget asked. She felt dowdier than ever in the same room with Ilene. Ilene's hair had been washed and was fashioned into a bun at the nape of her neck. She wore an exquisite wool hat pulled low on her brow and the coat that she'd worn the day she burst into the hotel. Confidence oozed out of her every movement as she carried her satchel to the door.

"Well, that's what Mabel called her when she told everyone how she'd made a mistake and come right into the hotel and then had to stay. Doc called her a blooming idiot who couldn't read," Allie Mae said.

Bridget could have hugged the girl for the last comment.

Ilene huffed. "When is the car arriving to take me to the station? Lord Almighty, I'm so glad to get out of here, I could shout."

"Ah, it's not a bad place to live. Folks are friendly

and kind. Don't get no better than Miss Bridget. If you had to get stuck in a hotel for a week, be thankful it was with her and not Mabel," Allie Mac said.

Ilene shot her a mean look and walked out the front door.

"How'd you live with that for a whole week?" Allie Mae whispered.

"I made her work. Oh, wait a minute. I forgot to pay her."

Allie Mae shook her head as if trying to dislodge a foreign idea. "She worked?"

Bridget pulled two envelopes from her pocket. She carried one out to the porch and handed it to Ilene. "That's seven dollars. A dollar a day and your room and board. You ever need a job working in a laundry, tell the proprietor to call me, and I'll give you a good reference."

"Why don't you drop dead? I'm made of good stock. I endured the torture, but I didn't like it, and I still don't like you. I'm just glad we'll never see each other again," Ilene said.

"All the same, a body never knows when catastrophe might come their way. Time might come along when you'd be glad to make those kinds of wages. You go on and have a wonderful life, Ilene."

Ilene tucked the envelope into her pocket and stepped off the porch and to the car, where Orville waited.

"So this is it, I guess," Wyatt said, so close behind Bridget that she jumped.

She held out the second envelope. "Your pay. I believe you'll find thirty dollars in there. I started to dock you a day's pay, since you never did kill the rat, but I couldn't do it, since you took such good care of me and Ella while I was ailing."

He held out his hand. "It's been an experience, Bridget."

She shook his hand, not amazed in the least that her heart fluttered at the touch of his skin against her palm. "Thank you, Wyatt, for all you've done around here. You are a good man."

"You are very welcome."

Bridget swallowed hard, but the lump in her throat wouldn't go down, so the little speech she'd worked on all night was in vain.

"You take care now," was all she could get out without tears.

"You do the same. You're ever in Alvord, Texas, look me up."

"What if you are in Healdton, Oklahoma?"

"Then look me up there," he said.

Ilene yelled at him that they were going to be late, and he let go of Bridget's hand.

He waved from the car window, and she held up a hand.

Then she went inside to settle back into her comfortable rut, where no one could ever hurt her again.

Allie Mae bombarded her with questions the minute she walked in the door. "We're doing pot roast today, right? You got the potatoes peeled, or should I start with them? And why are there nails in the walls?"

"Yes, this is Tuesday. Pot roast is in the oven, but I only made about half our usual amount, because it'll take a while for the customers to feel safe. Yes, please start peeling potatoes and scraping carrots. And the nails were for clotheslines."

"I'll have Orville take them down," Allie Mae said.

"No, leave them for a while."

Allie Mae looked at her strangely.

"Never know when we might want to use them again. This afternoon between dinner and supper we'll need to shake down the two used bedrooms upstairs and send the laundry out to be done. Or maybe if Orville is ready to work, he could do that this morning," she said.

Allie Mae nodded and followed Bridget to the kitchen.

Ilene and Wyatt sat together during the short ride to El Dorado. They did indeed make a lovely couple, and several people smiled at them, expecting they were newlyweds on their honeymoon.

When they reached the El Dorado station, Ilene stayed seated. "I appreciate your doing this for me," she said.

"Anything for a friend," he said.

She fluttered her eyelashes and flirted, happy to be back in her own realm of sanity. To her the past week had been nothing short of a week in an asylum. "It'll just make things so much easier. I don't think I'm going to marry Arty. I'm not so sure I'll ever marry. You've broken my heart, Wyatt."

"Ilene, I can't break your heart. That's a job for someone you truly love. When your heart is really hurting, you remember that I said that."

"If my heart is ever really hurting, I'll come around, and you can tell me that you told me so," she said.

"You'll have to come to Healdton, Oklahoma, then. I think that's where I'm going to settle," he said.

"God, you are stupid. You're right. You could never break my heart."

"Glad we got that settled. See you around probably. Just don't break my brother's heart while you are looking for the right rich man."

"Reuben? Oh, darlin', he's already a fading memory. And even if he was my heartthrob, I'd leave him alone. I never go back on my word."

"For that I owe you. Have a nice trip." He walked out of the train car and toward the nearest hotel. He'd spend the night and arrive in Alvord the next day. One day after Ilene reached her home in the next town on the line, Chico. That way no one in the area would ever know about the week they'd spent together at the Black Swan hotel in Huttig, Arkansas.

He checked into the hotel and picked up *Tom Sawyer.* He'd finished reading it to Bridget, so he started at the beginning again, looking up every few sentences to imagine the look on her face at a particular passage. One time he could have sworn he heard her giggle. He ordered dinner and supper brought to his room and didn't leave until the next morning. It was midafternoon when he stepped off the train in Alvord, where his youngest brother, Clayton, waited with a car to take him home.

Huge elm trees lined the lane from the road to the house. Black Angus cattle grazed what little grass they could find in February. Hay was scattered to supplement what was lacking. Several cars were parked in the oval driveway in front of the three-story brick home at the end of the lane. Evidently they'd all come home to welcome the prodigal back into their midst.

He squared his shoulders and walked into the foyer. Clayton led the way into the library, where his father sat behind the massive mahogany desk, his mother in a burgundy leather chair beside him. The rest of his brothers were scattered around the room. Everyone rose and crossed the room for handshakes, hugs, and welcomes.

Everything was fine now. He was home, and he'd forget the month in Huttig. It wouldn't be so hard after all. Already he'd gone five minutes without thinking of Ella and whether or not she was asleep in the crib he'd brought down from the attic. He pictured Bridget in the kitchen taking a pan of fresh yeast rolls from the oven. He shut his eyes and inhaled. When he opened them, he saw six people staring strangely at him.

"Pardon me. It's good to be home. I just had a flashback of hot rolls and thought I could smell them cooking in the oven."

"What happened at that hotel that you didn't tell me?" His mother gave him a scrutinizing look, starting at the tips of his shoes and traveling up to the top of his head. He needed a haircut in the worst way, but everything else appeared all right except for the lost look in her son's green eyes.

"Nothing. I've had a holiday, and I've made up my mind about what I'd like to do with my life. We'll discuss that later, Dad. Now, tell me what is new in Alvord?" He drew the attention away from himself. They all began to talk at once, but he didn't fool his mother one bit.

He had an hour with the family, then a two-hour business meeting with his father and mother where he told them what he wanted to do about settling in Healdton, Oklahoma, for a while.

"The oil boom is big in that area, and I think it would be good politics for us to have a representative right there. You remember Briar Nelson?"

His father nodded.

"Of course we remember Briar. Met him in Pennsylvania about a year ago. Had that lovely little girl I fell in love with," his mother, Dorothy, sighed.

"Well, he's transferred his whole operation to Healdton. He's married a wonderful lady, and his little girl adores her. I spent a few days there on my way to Little Rock and was on my way back home when I got delayed in Huttig," he said.

"And who is in Huttig?" Dorothy asked.

"No one in particular."

His father chuckled. "Then who is in Healdton?"

"Absolutely no one."

"Let's put this idea on paper and see how it looks. I'm thinking maybe it's a good one. Are you going there to run from something in Huttig?" Dorothy asked.

"No, I'm not running from anyone ever again."

"Then enjoy a week of getting back into the office groove, and we'll talk about it later," his father said.

Later that night he hung his coat up and saw the envelope Bridget had given him. He opened it to find thirty dollars, but the money meant less to him than the flowing handwriting on the envelope. He held it to his heart and wished he'd never left without her. But that was an impossible yearning, because she'd stated quite emphatically that she never intended to marry again. And there was the other thing also. She'd been married to a wealthy man and would probably always have the horrible fear that all rich, powerful men became abusive after the wedding.

He sat in a plush chair beside the window in his third-story suite of rooms and watched the moonbeams play across his legs. What was Ella doing right then? Was she already asleep? Was Bridget looking out her window at the same moon?

He fell asleep in the chair, only to dream of the three of them on the beach in Galveston. Bridget's face was aglow with delight because she'd finally seen the water for which she'd been named. A vast body that extended to the sunset.

Bridget was restless that night, more so than she'd been the first night Wyatt was gone from the hotel. She paced the floor and even went out onto the porch to watch the moon rise. If she had the nerve her sisters had, she would bundle Ella up and buy a ticket for Alvord, Texas. But she didn't, so she'd just have to get over her feelings and tie down her emotions.

She sat down in the cold rocking chair and pulled her legs up under her thick robe. "Maybe tomorrow will be easier. Surely it will. Each day will put more and more distance between us, and that will make it easier."

Somehow saying the words didn't help her to believe them at all.

Chapter Fourteen

Two weeks had passed, and still Bridget turned quickly when she heard a deep voice in the lobby. For barely a split second she thought Wyatt had come down from the attic or up from the basement for a midmorning cup of coffee and piece of pie or cake. But it was just Major Engram stopping by for a bit of gossip and a cup of coffee.

"Bring that baby over here and talk to an old man," he said.

Everything was caught up and ready for the first dinner rush. Tuesday was pot roast and chocolate pie. Wyatt's favorite, she remembered. She and Ella joined Major at a table where Allie Mae had set out a slab of pound cake covered in canned peaches and topped with whipped cream, along with a cup of coffee.

"That girl is going to do you proud," Major said.

"You think so?"

"I bet she and Orville could run this place."

"She's pretty young for that kind of responsibility."

"Well, honey, you ain't that much older than her and not a whit older than Orville. He's twenty this last week. Allie Mae told me so. And she's almost sixteen. Lots of sawmill wives that age around Huttig. They just need some experience, and you can give them lots of that."

Bridget wondered what Major was getting at but decided to let him have his time. He'd get around to telling her what was on his mind by the time he finished the cake.

"I suppose so," she said.

"You could take a few days off and go see one of your sisters and let them have a go at it. Hire Lizzy next door to come help Allie Mae in the kitchen. That youngest of hers is up and walking. She could watch him and work too," Major said.

"I'd have to give that a lot of thought."

"You do that. Woman needs to get out and around after being cooped up for weeks with no company except a hired hand and a fancy lady who can't read," Major said.

The seed had been planted, and by evening Bridget had already mentally packed and unpacked her suitcase a dozen times. Grace, Mississippi, kept playing through her mind, and she'd almost decided that a trip to see Alice might be the very thing she needed to bring her up out of the doldrums. A week in the country in a house instead of a hotel was so appealing that she picked up the stationery that evening to write Alice a long letter. But then Ella wanted attention, so Bridget picked up a book and sat down in the rocking chair. Folks would say she was daft for reading to a five-month-old baby, but the pictures in the book intrigued Ella, and Bridget remembered the happy times when she'd sat in her mother's lap and listened to stories.

Ella fell asleep somewhere in the middle of the book, and Bridget put her to bed. The springs squeaked just slightly in the crib, and her first thought was that she'd have to tell Wyatt to take the mattress out and oil them the next day.

She paced the floor and wished Major hadn't stopped by that day. Until he mentioned it, she hadn't realized how much she wanted and needed to get away from the hotel. The walls began to creep inward, and the room got smaller and smaller. She grabbed a quilt and headed for the porch. The night air in February was still very cold, but she could endure it if she could just be outside.

The moon hung low in the sky, visible through the pine needles as a pale yellow ball. Alice could paint that and make it so real, a person could feel the chill of the night air when they looked at it. An owl hooted off in the distance, but it was too early for tree frogs or crickets, so the poor old owl had to present a solo.

She wrapped the quilt around her like a shawl and sat down on a rocking chair. The idea of giving Allie Mae and Orville a trial run at the hotel was tempting, but the place had never been open a single day without an O'Shea in attendance. She weighed pros and cons and an hour later made her decision. If Lizzy would agree to work, she would go. If not, it wasn't meant to be.

At nine-thirty the next morning she sent Orville over to Lizzy's house to ask if she had time to drop by that day. Lizzy followed him back, carrying one little fellow in her arms and a two-year-old girl tugging on her hem.

"The rest of the brood is in school, thank goodness. What do you need, Bridget?" she said bluntly. Lizzy didn't listen to gossip. She didn't spread gossip. She could scarcely bear to be in the same neighborhood with Mabel. She was blunt, and she spoke her mind. She was a tall, rawboned woman who somehow missed being ugly and was quite attractive with her brown hair and big brown eyes.

Bridget started to tell the whole story from how the flu had left her feeling antsy and so on and so on, but instead she took a leaf from Lizzy's book. "I'm needing to go away for a week, and I need your help. Allie Mae and Orville know how to run this place, but they need some help, and I'd like to hire you to do that."

"I've got these two littl'uns at home. . . ." Lizzy said.

"Bring them with you. We take care of Ella and run the place. Orville can help when he's not got something else going," Bridget said.

"You comfortable with that, Allie Mae?"

"Yes, ma'am. I'd just love to see if me and Orville

can take care of the Black Swan with your help. Someday me and Orville want to have our own place just like this."

"I can sure use the money right now. Sawmill is cutting back the hours, and Roy is only getting three days a week now," Lizzy said.

"I'll hire him to work the days he's not working at the mill," Bridget said.

"But . . ." Orville paled.

"I'm not firing you. I'm hiring an older man to give you some help," Bridget said quickly.

"I can use it. I like Roy. We'll work good together. Been meanin' to ask you about that shed out back. I'd like to tear it down and rebuild it this spring," Orville said.

"We can talk about that later. So it's set. Can you start work tomorrow morning?" Bridget asked Lizzy.

"That would be good. I'll tell Roy he's on duty over here when he's not at the mill. And I thank you, Bridget, for thinking of me. You are a good neighbor."

"So are you," Bridget said. The heavy weight in her chest hadn't lifted as she'd thought it would when she had everything finalized. Maybe it would when she had spent a week with Alice and Ira.

Wyatt fooled all of his family but his mother. Something wasn't right with her son, and she had an idea it had to do with a woman. She gave him two weeks to get it straightened out on his own and then called a business meeting with him in the library. She was a lovely lady with gray hair, green eyes, soft features, and a small frame. When she entered a room, it was with unexplained force for such a sweet-looking, refined lady.

That morning was no exception. Wyatt sat in a comfortable leather chair and scanned the titles of books on two walls of the library. He and his brothers had been encouraged to read from the time they could hold a book and make out the words. By the time they started school, all five of them could read children's books. Reuben was reading the newspaper by then, but he'd always been the most intelligent of the tribe, which was what his father called the brothers.

Dorothy Ferguson breezed into the room and sat behind the desk. "We have decided that you should open an office in Healdton. It was an excellent idea you came up with, and our oil business is booming, literally. We could send someone to serve as head of the company, but you have a desire to go, and it would be beneficial to have you take over the business in that whole area. Basically you'll have an office with a staff of three. Choose them well. A good accountant. I'd suggest Matthew O'Malley. He's served the company well the past ten years, and I think he'd be willing to relocate his family to Oklahoma."

"What do you think about Harry for a field man?"

"Harry is your best friend, and you'd work well together. It would do Harry good to get out of Alvord. Offer him the job. But you need at least two men and then rig bosses under each of them. I was thinking about your brother, Brendon, for the other field man."

Wyatt nodded slowly. "Brendon and I work well together, and he's always been one who likes to be out in the field rather than in the office. He also gets along well with Harry. It could work well."

"Then you can go ahead with your plans to hire them and make your move in the next few days. We've already sent an agent to the area, and he's bought a building on the main street of town for your office. The sign will be hung at the end of the week. Your first job had better be to find a place to live." Dorothy eased into that part of her strategy.

"I'd like something outside of town on a few acres. Maybe a small farmhouse," he said.

"For you and your brother?" Dorothy asked.

Wyatt sighed.

"Don't you think you'd better unload that baggage you've been toting around for two weeks, son?"

"You're not going to like it. Ilene said you'd throw a fit," he said.

"Ilene doesn't know me, so her opinion means nothing. If I don't like it, I'll damn well tell you I don't, but it won't be because she says so. That woman is a package of trouble waiting to happen. Besides, when have you seen her? I heard she threw Arty over too and ran off to her sister's for some time to think about things. She just got home to Chico yesterday."

"It's a long story," Wyatt said.

Dorothy settled deeper into the chair. "I've got all morning."

"I was sworn to secrecy. It can't leave this room, or else she'll go after Reuben. Even though he's smart, he's not so good with women," Wyatt said.

"I can keep a secret, but I'll see that woman in the grave before I see her married to one of my sons," Dorothy said.

Wyatt knew he was a sinking ship before he even began to talk.

He told the story of why he'd really let himself be coerced into a job at the Black Swan, about the flu and Ilene barging into the hotel. He told about Ralph's disappearance and the divorce and Ella. He finished up by telling his mother that he and Ilene had made a deal, and he'd just broken his end of it.

"Sounds to me like you've fallen in love with an Irish lass by the name of Bridget O'Shea," Dorothy said.

"A divorced Irish lass who might or might not have killed her abusive husband and who has stated several times she'll never have another one," he said.

"Did you tell her how you feel?"

"No, I did not. She'd throw it back in my face so fast, it would make my head swim."

"Way I see it is that you need to go to Healdton and find a home. Then you need to take two days and go back to Huttig and tell her that you are in love with her. You never know what she'll say until you tell her. Women can fool you, son. Look at how Ilene hoodwinked you."

"You would be comfortable with a daughter-in-law like that?"

"She sounds like a fighter and a lovely lady. Besides, I'd be getting a granddaughter. That alone is worth a lot, Wyatt. And if she's in love with you, then you will change that child's name to Ferguson. I'm just tickled that she's Irish."

"Never thought of that," Wyatt said.

"Your father will be ecstatic that one of you boys brought good Irish blood into the family. You've got lots of work to do this next week. And tell Briar Nelson and his daughter hello for me when you get there. I'll come visit in a few months, and I'll expect to meet his wife then. Don't disappoint me."

Still unable to believe his mother was accepting the notion of a divorced woman for a prospective daughter-in-law, Wyatt asked, "In work or in my personal life?"

"Both. I can't wait to meet Bridget. Don't mess it up," she said on her way out of the office, leaving him sitting in stunned silence.

It was a glorious week on Alice and Ira's farm. Bridget planned another holiday in the early summer to Little Rock. She and Ella could travel often now that she had a good crew to take care of the hotel. She arrived in

Huttig on a Tuesday afternoon at three-thirty and re-membered when she got off the train that she had forgot-ten to drop Orville a note to pick her up.

"Oh, well, it's a lovely day, isn't it, Ella? The sun is bright, and it's not too warm. A nice day for a walk through the town. We'll send Orville back for our bag-gage later." She headed into the station to tell the man there to set her cases aside for Orville.

A long line waited at the counter, but she wasn't in a hurry, so she sat down on a bench that barely had room for her on the end. The line held her attention, so she didn't even notice who she'd sat down beside until she was spoken to.

"Well, Bridget O'Shea, did you finally decide to come back to Huttig where you belong? I'd thought maybe you were the one who was going to show some good sense. Lord knows you should after the way your husband treated you. But it appears that you are just like your sisters and lacking in good sense too. Where have you been? Off chasing some man like they did? Only thing that saved their reputations was the fact that the men did marry them." Mabel went on and on, scarcely stopping for breath between sentences.

"I went to visit Alice for a week, not that it's a bit of your business, ma'am." Bridget stood up and started the long walk to the hotel. Surely the clerk would know to set her bags aside without being told. If she'd listened to another of Mabel's tirades, she would have kicked her into the hole with Ralph. Good grief, she'd just spent a whole week and never even thought of the man, and when she got back to Huttig, the first rattle out of the bucket had his name on it.

"I think we'll go visit Catherine next week. Maybe tomorrow. It's plain I'm going to have to listen to gossip every day in this place," she whispered to Ella.

Allie Mae was sweeping the front porch when she arrived. She threw the broom down and met her in the front yard with a hug. "Miss Bridget, you're home!"

"Everything go all right?" Bridget asked.

"Went fine. I just missed you is all. Lizzy is a good woman, and, man, she can clean and cook, but I missed having you and Ella around." Allie Mae kept an arm around Bridget as they all three trooped into the hotel.

"Orville, please take the car and go pick up my bags at the station. I should have sent a letter telling you my arrival time, but I forgot," she said when they were in the lobby.

Lizzy wiped her hands on a dishcloth as she crossed the floor to stand in front of Bridget. "I like the work. Roy likes the hotel. You get tired of it, we'd like to buy it if we can."

Bridget was set back. "Oh, my, I never thought of such a thing."

"Well, if you do, then we'd like first chance at it. Until then I'd like to apply for a full-time job here. It suits me and Roy. He's sure likin' it better'n workin' the sawmill," Lizzy said.

"I'll keep that in mind," Bridget said. "Now, what

can I do? It's Tuesday again. Pot roast. Same as the day I left."

"It's all done, and the kitchen is cleaned. You and Ella had your dinner yet? We can set you up at a table," Lizzy said.

"We ate on the train, but thank you. I would like to have a little nap and I know she's tired. Reckon it would be all right if we hid away in our quarters for the rest of the day?"

"It'd be fine. I'm paid through the whole day," Lizzy said.

Bridget slept all afternoon and into the evening. Ella's fussing woke her at dusk, and she arose to find an empty hotel. Her help had all gone home, and there were no guests. However, there had been three men and a family of four who'd rented rooms for a few nights while she was in Grace, so the hotel business was picking up.

She rooted around and found enough leftover roast to make a sandwich for herself and mashed potatoes and carrots for Ella. They shared a piece of chocolate pie, Ella getting most of the filling. She picked up the baby and was headed across the dark lobby when the front door opened.

"Roy?" she asked the tall shadow.

"Who is Roy?" Wyatt asked.

"The man who helps me. What are you doing here?" Bridget's chest tightened.

He pulled a chain and turned on the lights. She was

even more beautiful with all that gorgeous hair streaming down her back. Ella had grown in the three weeks he'd been gone, but her eyes said she remembered him.

"Can we sit?" he asked.

She was glad to do just that.

"I'm living in Healdton now, as I told you I'd like to do. My folks let me take over the entire oil operation. It's hard work, but I love it. My brother, Brendon, came to Healdton with me. He's a field man—never did like staying inside and would die if anyone put him in an office. And my friend Harry too. He's the other field man. I've got an accountant who serves as a secretary-type fellow. Good family man who was glad to relocate with me."

"That's good," she murmured. She wanted to scoot down on the settee until her body was plastered right up next to his. She wanted to feel his lips on hers again. "But what brings you to Huttig? Is there oil here too?"

"No, something even more precious," he said.

"And that would be?"

"You and Ella. I've got something to say, and please hear me out before you say no, Bridget. You've made it clear that you'll never marry again. . . ."

"Can't do it. Can't hear you out on that one because I've changed my mind on the marryin' thing. It was wrong of me to judge all men by one sorry piece of humanity. Now go on."

"Okay, then. In that month I was here, I fell in love with you and Ella. I want to marry you. I want to adopt

Ella. I want you to come to Healdton with me and live on the farm I've bought there. It's a little three-bedroom, two-story house, and I'm having modern plumbing put in while I'm gone. There's a rosebush on one side and a root cellar and a barn. I plan to run some Angus cattle on the land as a sideline," he said.

She giggled.

"What's so funny?"

"You just asked me to marry you and then told me about a rosebush and a root cellar. I think you are very nervous," she said.

"You'll never know how nervous I am right now. My whole life, happiness, and future depend on your answer, so I'd tell you about the wild bunnies and the oak trees if it would make you say yes," he said.

"I've been miserable without you too, Wyatt. I went to Alice's for a week, trying to outrun my feelings. I'll marry you because I love you so much, it hurts, and I'll let you adopt Ella, but her name remains Ella O'Shea."

"Ella O'Shea Ferguson?"

"I can handle that," she said.

"Did you just say yes? Really, did you?" he asked.

"I did. I'm selling the hotel and marrying you. Now you decide when."

"Tomorrow?"

"Why so quick?"

"I've got two days—tomorrow and the next one—before I have to go back to the office. I don't want to live another day without you. It'll be a year before I can take you on a proper honeymoon to the ocean, but I promise that when the business is stable, I'll take you there and anywhere else you want to go every single year."

"When is the next train to El Dorado?" she asked.

"Tomorrow morning."

"I'll get my things packed. Can you make arrangements to have some of my personal effects shipped to Healdton?"

"I can do that. Why do you want to go to El Dorado?"

"Because I'm selling the hotel to Lizzy and Roy. I need to talk to them and set a price and then go talk to my banker."

"You're making those kinds of decisions this quickly?" he asked.

"Yes, I am, but it's not all that quickly. My heart has known for weeks how much I love you. Now, would you please stop talking and kiss me, Wyatt Ferguson? I think a marriage proposal is supposed to be romantic. This has been more like a business deal," she said.

He quickly moved down the settee and gathered her into his arms, Ella wiggling between them. He tilted her chin back with one finger and looked into the prettiest aqua eyes he'd ever seen. He'd always heard that when a man was about to die, his whole life flashed before him. He wasn't aware that it could happen the same way when two hearts and souls were bound together for eternity, but it did.

He liked what he saw in that second about his future with Bridget. When his lips met hers and the sparks flew around them, the heavy load he'd been carrying was lifted from his chest.

Bridget was truly in love with Wyatt. She'd figured that out weeks ago and had tried in vain to outrun it.

When he kissed her, every fiber of her body knew what passion truly was and that it would always be that way with Wyatt.

Life had given her a second chance.

She grabbed on to it and vowed to never let go.

Epilogue

Spring 1960

Bright sunshine lit up the white streaks in Catherine's shoulder-length dark burgundy hair that fine spring morning. Alice had a little gray salting the short red hair she wore waved back away from her face. Bridget's long strawberry blond hair, worn twisted up in an elegant French roll, had no gray.

They'd driven from El Dorado in Alice's new baby-blue Cadillac. Every year the three sisters came home to Huttig to see about the graves, and they came alone. No husbands or children were allowed. Back in the twenties, when Lizzy and Roy owned the Black Swan, they had stayed there. In the thirties, Lizzy and Roy sold the place to Orville and Allie Mae and moved to Shreveport to buy a bigger hotel. In the forties, Orville and Allie Mae sold out to a family with enough kids to fill an orphanage.

They kept the restaurant open for a few years until their children were grown and gone and then sold the Black Swan to another family, who closed the business and made it a home. By the late forties, it was going to ruin, and in 1955 someone bought the land and tore the hotel down. An institution gone after only fifty-three years.

By then fire had claimed the Commercial, and the town of Huttig didn't even have a hotel. No matter what it still had or didn't have, it was home to the O'Shea sisters, and they came every year to pay their respects to Patrick and Ella O'Shea.

That morning in 1960, Alice opened the trunk of the, Caddy, and they took out three folding lawn chairs. Alice picked up a jug of sweet tea. Bridget brought out a brown paper bag full of oatmeal cookies. Catherine grabbed the sack with the paper cups and napkins. They carried the items to their parents' graves and unfolded the chairs in a semicircle. Catherine sat in the first one, Alice in the middle, Bridget on the other end.

Catherine handed Alice three cups, and she filled them with cold sweet tea. Catherine placed a napkin on each of their laps, and Bridget laid out three cookies each. It had been the same for forty years. They had tea at the cemetery. Pulled any weeds that might be threatening to take over the grave sites. Enjoyed the wild white daisies, blue forget-me-nots, and tiny purple hyacinth that bloomed in among the jonquils. And talked about the days when they were little girls and their parents ran the Black Swan hotel. They remembered citizens of the town who had passed on and were laid to rest in the cemetery. They wondered if Mabel would ever die or if she'd live forever because God and Lucifer hadn't settled the fight over who had to take her, because neither wanted her. The woman was eighty-five, and her gossip vine still flourished in Huttig, Arkansas.

"Do you feel sixty yet?" Alice asked Bridget.

"Does it feel different than fifty-nine?" She answered with a question.

"Not so much," Catherine said. "Two years ago, when I turned sixty, I thought the world would surely come to an end, but the sun came up, and life went right on."

"We've come through a lot and seen even more," Alice said.

"Wars and rumors of wars." Catherine smiled.

"Husbands, kids, and now grandkids," Alice said.

"Momma took good care of us, didn't she?" Bridget said.

"She did. She'd be glad for this day, and she'd love all three of her sons-in-law. And wouldn't she have spoiled all the grandchildren?" Catherine nodded.

"You ever sorry for any of the ways things turned out?" Bridget asked Catherine, who was still beautiful at sixty-two—taller than the other two women, back straight, head held high, and a ready smile on her face. Her green eyes still sparkled when she was happy and turned dark when she was angry.

"Never one day, and I'm not sorry for forty years of not telling our secret either," she said.

"Me either," Alice said. "Not that Ira would care anyway. But I'm not sorry." Alice had grown into her own with the passage of time. No more was she the odd, flighty girl who wasn't "quite right in the head." These days she was an eccentric but famous artist whose paintings were in high demand. Only the very rich could afford an Alice McNewel to hang in their living room.

"You? Would you do anything differently?" Catherine asked Bridget.

She slowly shook her head. "Back when Wyatt first came to the hotel, I was still afraid of everything. He helped bring me out of my shell. Looking back, I think fate played a big part in our lives that spring forty years ago. If Momma hadn't gotten the flu, I wouldn't have had the nerve to come home against Ralph's wishes. That's what brought him to Huttig that night and set the whole thing into motion. If he hadn't died that night, Quincy wouldn't have come looking for him, and you wouldn't have found the love of your life, Catherine. If Quincy hadn't arrived when he did, then you wouldn't have been married when Ira came back from the war. Out of respect and obligation, you would have married him, and Alice would have been cheated out of the love of her life. If you'd both been there, the rat that sent me to town to find someone to help me at the hotel wouldn't have been a problem, because you would have taken care of it, Catherine. If I hadn't gone off in a temper fit to find a man with big feet to kill the rat, I wouldn't have met Wyatt and wound up with the love of my life.

So, no, I wouldn't change a thing. Everything happened as it should. We've had good lives right up to this glorious, happy day."

"Whew! That was some speech, but it's true," Alice said.

"She always was the mystical one with the lightest eyes and hair. Papa said she was the one with the gift," Catherine said.

"Gift of foresight or gab?" Alice teased.

"Must be gab. You got the foresight," Bridget said.

Alice looked at Catherine. "But you were the strong one."

"Not that night. I think you were the strong one then," Catherine answered.

"Don't be giving me any credit. I just saw what we needed to do to keep Bridget from going to jail. You all would have figured it out in time." Alice smiled.

"Not fast enough. It took all three of us working until nearly morning to get that job done," Catherine said.

Bridget patted Alice's arm. "And, darlin', you were the one who sent me and Catherine home in the car so it would be in the right place at daylight. Remember, you said no one would think anything about your being out so early? I can still remember sitting in the lobby and hearing you whistle as you meandered down the road that morning. Lord, what a nightmare."

"Well, you didn't need to have that memory of dirt going in on top of him, even if he was meaner than a snake," Alice said.

"See? *You* were the strong one," Catherine said.

"For just that once maybe air was stronger than earth and water." Alice nodded.

Bridget nibbled the edge of a cookie much as she had that morning when Quincy stepped out of the sheriff's car and announced that he was hunting for Ralph Contiello, dead or alive. "Whatever made you think of putting him there instead of the garden or the basement?"

"I knew someone would come looking someday. They'd dig up everything that had loose dirt around our hotel, so we couldn't put his body there. We sure couldn't put it in the river, or it would wash up eventually. So I just thought, where do dead bodies belong? Besides, the dirt was still fresh and easy to dig. They'd only covered Momma up that very morning," Alice said.

"Do you think Momma has minded all these years?" Bridget looked at the tombstone with her mother and father's names engraved on the granite.

"Honey, I figure she's held on to him real tight. She'd do anything for her girls. Even in death she helped us. I've got to admit, though, that putting him down there on top of her coffin was the hardest thing I ever did," Alice said.

"Why?" Bridget asked.

"Throwing evil on top of good?" Catherine asked.

"That's right. I asked her forgiveness and then kicked his sorry body down into the hole, filled it up, and hid the shovel. Two days later I drove the car back down here under the pretense of visiting Momma's grave and put the shovel in the trunk. I was sure glad all three shovels were lined up in the shed when Quincy came sniffing around," Alice said.

"Forty years and we visit every year, but we never even talked about it until now," Bridget said.

"Maybe it took that long before it didn't scare the liver out of us," Alice said.

"Maybe so," Bridget said.

Catherine looked down the row at Bridget. "You're not sorry?"

"Hell, no. Think of the life Ella has had because of that night. Wyatt has been her father since she was five months old. And all my four sons. I didn't think I could raise a boy child, but it wasn't so difficult," Bridget declared. "But, just in case, let's promise again that we'll take the secret with us to our graves."

"What secret?" Catherine's eyes twinkled.

Alice reached out, and they took her hands.

Earth, air, and water.

Nothing could shake them if they stuck together.